DEVOTIONAL STORIES FOR TEENS

MY FATHER OWNS THIS PLACE

ABOUT GETTING ALONG IN GOD'S WORLD

GARY B. SWANSON

D0675001

REVIEW AND HERALD® PUBLISHING ASSOCIATION
HAGERSTOWN, MD 21740

Copyright © 1997 by
Review and Herald® Publishing Association
International copyright secured

The author assumes full responsibility for the accuracy of all facts and quotations as cited in this book.

This book was
Edited by Jeannette R. Johnson
Designed by Helcio Deslandes
Desktop technician: Shirley M. Bolivar
Cover design by Willie S. Duke
Typeset: 12/14 Galliard

PRINTED IN U.S.A.

01 00 99 98 97 5 4 3 2

R&H Cataloging Service
Swanson, Gary B.
My father owns this place: devotional stories for teens about getting along in God's world.

1. Teenagers—Prayerbooks and devotions—English.
I. Title.

242.63

ISBN 0-8280-1252-0

CONTENTS

1 ALVIN THE TERRIBLE

Day 1: My first day as a counselor at Pine Springs Ranch is over, and I'm so tired my hair aches. It took until fireside time tonight to get all the kids happily situated in their cabins. All afternoon they shouted and pushed one another around and cried because they wanted the top bunk or they were homesick or they didn't get in the same cabin as their friends. Assuring that everybody is happy on the first day of summer camp could make for a promising career in diplomacy.

It looks now, however, as though everybody's finally satisfied. The five boys in my cabin have fallen asleep. Their faces look almost angelic. It's hard to believe they were bouncing like Ping-Pong balls all over the cabin an hour ago. I thought they'd never go to sleep.

So here I am, jotting down these few thoughts by flashlight. Lights out was more than an hour ago. If it weren't so cold at night, the kids would probably have never crawled into their sleeping bags. I must make an effort to be more thankful for small favors.

Day 2: I came up here this summer because I want to be a teacher or youth counselor. At least I think I do. Mrs. Sanders, our school counselor, suggested that summer camp would be a good experience and would give me an idea of whether I really want to go on with this kind of work. When I see her again in September, I'll have a little advice for her! More than once today I've regretted turning down that nice, quiet summer job Mr. Estevez offered me at the library.

Now I know why people send their children to camp: it's a matter of self-preservation. Alvin is a perfect example. He isn't really a bad little guy; I can see that already. He's like an accident looking for a place to happen, and he never sits still for more than 15 seconds. When the rest of us are making up our bunks, he's running to the lodge for breakfast. When the other kids are finishing their French toast, he's off to the animal cages. I can't get him to stop. Most-frequently-asked question in Cabin C-5: "Has anyone seen Alvin?"

Day 3: I woke this morning in the dark with Alvin standing next to my bed, fiddling with my flashlight. He was fully clothed and apparently ready for the day.

"What do you want, Alvin?"

"I'm going out to the campfire place to start a fire."

"No way!"

"I'm cold," he said, with an exaggerated shiver.

"Well, what are you doing out of bed?"

"It's getting light. I thought we were supposed to get up early, like buffalo hunters."

"Not until 6:00," I said. "I think the buffalo are still in bed too."

"Well, may I get in with you?"

"Are you kidding? There isn't room for both of us in my sleeping bag."

By then I was completely awake, so I suggested we take a walk until the others got up in half an hour. Alvin flew out the door with my flashlight before I could pull my pants on.

I caught up with him on the pathway to the cafeteria. He was trying to turn on a faucet that had had its handle removed.

"How come this faucet doesn't have a handle?" he asked.

"I guess it's used only at certain times, and they don't want someone to come along and maybe leave it running."

"Why would anybody do that?"

"Well, why are you trying to turn it on now?"

"Just wanted to fill my canteen. I'm thirsty."

"We'll fill your canteen up at the cafeteria," I said, reaching for my flashlight. Suddenly throwing his arms up in front of his face, Alvin dropped the flashlight and the canteen. "What's the matter?" I asked.

"I thought you were going to hit me!"

"What for?"

He shrugged matter of factly. "I don't know."

Day 4: I had hoped this journal would be a place where I could record my serene musings about the beautiful natural surroundings here, the scream of a far-off eagle, the feel of wet grass on my boots in the early morning, the wind sighing in the pines—sort of a Walden of my very own. But it looks, instead, as though my every musing is to be centered on Alvin the Terrible—that's what the rest of the counselors have begun to call him, and not entirely without reason.

This morning he dropped a whole basin of forks all over the cafeteria floor, soapsuds and hot water and all. A boy from Cabin A-14 slipped in the soapy water and cut his lip.

"Can't you keep an eye on that kid?" yelled the cook.

"He was only trying to help, Mr. Curry."

"Well, let him help somebody else; I've got enough to do around here without cleaning up that kind of mess!"

"We'll clean it up, Mr. Curry, and I'll see to it that Alvin is no trouble to you anymore."

It was a promise I don't know how in the world I'll keep, but Mr. Curry seemed appeased. He is really a nice guy, but the pressure of preparing food for 200 kids gets to him at times.

Day 5: Halfway through this camp session, and I wonder sometimes if I'll last. Actually, today wasn't as bad as the rest because I had the whole afternoon to myself while the kids went canoeing.

And when they got back, they were so tired they fell asleep right after fireside time—even Alvin.

He's really a cute little guy, in a ragged sort of way. I can't get him to comb his hair; it sticks out like straw where he has slept on it wrong. And he pays almost as little attention to his clothes. This morning I caught him on his way to breakfast wearing a holey pair of jeans and a wrinkled pajama top.

"Where's your shirt, Alvin?"

"This is it."

"Come on, Alvin, that's the top to your pajamas."

"Well, it looks like a shirt, doesn't it? Nobody'll ever notice."

"I noticed! Now get back to the cabin and find a shirt to wear."

When he got to breakfast, he was wearing a sweatshirt inside out and so wrinkled and dirty that I wondered if I should have let him wear the pajama top after all. "He's just a kid," I kept muttering to myself. "I can't let him get to me."

Day 6: It scares me a little to consider it, but I'm beginning to think the way Alvin does. Three times today I anticipated what he was going to do and headed him off.

When he was going out the door for breakfast this morning, I flagged him down and made him go wash his face—probably for the first time this week, maybe in his entire life. I know he did it this morning, though, because he came back to the cabin with the water dripping from his chin. He'd forgotten his face towel. I don't think I was cut out to be a camp counselor.

Day 7: I have to admit that I had a bad feeling since early this morning that today was going to be rough. The plan was to take the kids on a four-mile hike to Cedar Lake, let them swim for an hour, cook lunch over an open fire, and then hike the four miles back to the ranch. Piece of cake, right?

Everything went as scheduled until we started lunch. I had just finished showing the Cabin C-5 ping pong balls how to build a fire, using pine needles to get it started, and I really should have noticed Alvin's unusually rapt attention to what I was saying.

Sometime later, while I was busy cleaning up, Alvin returned from a nearby grove of pines with a huge armload of needles. He dropped them on the fire, turning it instantly into an inferno, popping and sailing sparks in all directions. Two or three pine trees stood close by, and it's a miracle none of them caught fire.

While I stood there, two quick-thinking counselors hastily shoveled dirt onto the fire, smothering it enough to keep it out of the trees. I looked for Alvin when the excitement died down and found him almost in a trance. His eyes were wide and his lips were trembling, and for the first time this week I felt sorry for him. I was really going to chew him out, but couldn't bring myself to do it when I saw how frightened he was.

I reached out to him to give him a hug. For the second time this week, he ducked as if I were going to hit him, and I realized that here was a kid who was a little too used to being slapped around. *Maybe,* I thought, *this kid lives at home with an adult who is even more terrible than he is!*

"I'm not going to hit you, Alvin," I said.

He looked at me curiously but wouldn't allow himself within reach.

Day 8: I thought after yesterday's fire episode at Cedar Lake that Alvin would be a new person this morning, but that wasn't to be, at least outwardly. It takes a little more than a near forest fire, I guess, to convince a 9-year-old that he should comb his hair in the morning. He acts as though he has forgotten that only yesterday he nearly burned the entire San Bernardino National Forest to the ground.

Well, tomorrow Alvin goes home, and I won't have to worry about him anymore. I sure hope the batch of kids that come in next week are less exuberant.

Day 9: This day didn't end exactly the way I expected it to. Just before getting on the bus, Alvin ran up to me.

"Are you going to be here again next summer?"

"I don't know," I said. "That's a long way off."

"Well, I hope you are. You're OK. *You* understand."

He ran off to the bus before I had a chance to respond. Actually, now that I think about it, that's what Alvin's been doing to me for a week—running off before I can respond. I wrote in yesterday's entry that when Alvin leaves I won't have to worry about him anymore. Not true. I will be worrying about him—about why a 9-year-old kid would involuntarily duck his head any time an adult reaches out to him. For the first time since I met Alvin the Terrible, I think I could face him again next summer.

2 BACK ON TRACK

Tom retched again as the car lurched through another pothole. He glowered at his sister, who was driving, grim and wordless, toward home. "Slow down, will ya, Paige! Can't you see I'm sick?"

"Yeah, I can see you're sick," Paige snapped, "and I can smell it too. You reek!"

Tom moaned and laid his throbbing head back against the headrest. As the car bounced and shuddered down Carmichael Avenue, the old familiar scenes of Long's Drugstore and the Safeway supermarket melded into a surrealistic swirl of color. "Oh, man," he groaned, "am I sick!"

"Of course you're sick. You think you have to tell me about it? For more than a year now I've been covering for you. You go out after school with those so-called friends of yours, find a case of beer somewhere, get sick all over yourself, and then call for me. If it weren't for my coming to get you and washing your filthy clothes before Mom and Dad get home from work, they'd have found out long ago. And then where would you be?"

A foolish smile played across Tom's face. He knew his sister's gruffness wouldn't last. She never had been able to stay angry with him for long. He thought back to the time when he was 6 years old and threw his soccer ball into her bedroom and broke the leg of one of her prized glass unicorns. Even then she'd gotten over it.

Tom's smile faded as quickly as it had appeared. "I'm sorry, Paige. I don't like myself like this either. I'll do better. This is the last time. I promise."

Paige glanced at Tom and sighed deeply. Tears rimmed her long eyelashes in silver. "Oh, Tom. You've said that so many times. When are you going to admit that you have a bigger problem than we can handle—even together? I can't keep rescuing you like this. Sooner or later something really bad is going to happen. Unless you do something about your problem, it'll eat you up. Give Mom and Dad a chance to help."

Bitter resentment flared up in Tom's throat and tears came to his eyes. Nobody—not even Paige—understood his problems. All his parents cared about was working all week and going to church.

But when he was drinking with his friends, nothing mattered. He could forget his D's and F's in school, the disapproval of his teachers, and his sister's nagging.

He *had* tried—several times. But always the

brutal logic had come back: Even if I can make it through a day or two without a beer, I'll probably drink one the next day, or the next. It'll keep coming back till it gets me. It always does.

Tom was fully angry and disgusted now—at himself, at his parents, even at Paige. He glared at his sister as she slowed the car to a stop at the Twelfth Street railroad crossing. "Why are we stopping here?" Tom demanded.

Paige laughed and shook her head. "Because a train's coming."

"That isn't fair," Tom muttered. "We were here first. The train should have to wait for us. Doesn't anyone understand that I'm sick and need to get home?"

"It'll be only a couple minutes, Tom. You know we stop here all the time, and the train is never long. You're not making any sense. Please try to be patient—"

Tom snatched the door handle back and swung the car door open. The harsh clanging of the railroad crossing bell pounded all the louder in his ears. *Somehow,* he decided, *I'm going to stop that train. We were here first!*

He lurched uncertainly forward, ducked under the crossing bar, and before Paige's horrified eyes took a stand between the two ribbons of steel. The train, only blocks away, let out a harsh, grinding screech. Tom could already feel the surging vibration of the huge engine through the ties. But in his swirling, sickening world, he had no doubt that he could stop the train pounding down the tracks toward him.

Then at the last moment fear froze him in place. What if the train did not, or could not, stop? What if—

The train whistle drowned out everything, filling Tom's head with a throbbing finality. He could see the huge, black hulk of the engine about to swallow him—and then his sister's frightened face was next to him. There was a scream, an overwhelming shock, and then a sifting silence.

An image flitted mysteriously across Tom's vision, a fuzzy, white figure that silently disappeared and then formed again. He knew he was waking and, strangely, this felt to him as if it were a great accomplishment.

The white figure gradually took the form of a nurse, who was busily tucking in the sheets at the foot of his bed. Tom tried to move, to lift his head, but pain flashed through his body and he groaned.

The nurse straightened up. "Well, hello there! You've been a long time coming around. Is there anything I can get you?"

Tom shook his head, and even that hurt. He reached up and ran his fingers over his heavily bandaged head. "It *should* hurt," the nurse smiled. "You've got a serious brain concussion, and you were very nearly killed."

Just as he was about to ask what had happened to him, the memory of the accident drifted back to him in disconnected waves and images. Then he remembered Paige.

Tom lay still for quite a time, wondering

about Paige, before he could muster the courage to ask about her. Surely, he thought, she must have been killed. He and his drinking were to blame. Tears warmed his eyes as he remembered her words: "Sooner or later . . ."

Finally he asked, "What happened to my sister?"

The nurse smiled and patted his hand. "She's going to make it. She very nearly lost a foot, but the doctors say she'll be walking again in a few months."

"May I see her?"

The nurse laughed. "As beaten up as you are, I'll be surprised if you can move at all for a couple days. And I think she's still in the recovery room right now anyway. What about your parents? Don't you want to see them?"

Tom turned his face toward the window at his bedside. "I don't think they'll want to see me."

"They were here all night—both of them on their knees, praying at your bedside. They left only a few minutes ago to get some breakfast."

"Do they know how it happened?"

The nurse nodded. And then, as if she were reading his mind, she said, "When the chips are down, parents are usually pretty understanding."

"I hope so," Tom said.

The nurse patted him on the arm. "You'll see," she said.

3 CHANGE OF HEART

"You're kidding!" Kristy said.

Maris shook her head. "No, I really mean it. I wasn't elected to anything this time."

Kristy still wasn't sure that Maris was telling her the truth. She closed her locker and looked intently at Maris. "You've been a class officer every year since sixth grade," she said. "You were president twice."

Maris swept a strand of straight black hair back from her forehead and shrugged wearily. "I guess now it's someone else's turn." She gathered her books, grabbed her sweater, and headed for the front door. It was difficult to hide her feelings from Kristy, and she had to admit to herself that it did hurt not to be elected to something for the first time in four years. She wondered what it all meant.

"You know what I think?" Kristy said. "I think

this has happened because of some of the things you tried to do last year. I've warned you that sometimes you let your being a Christian get in the way of having a little fun—like the time you tried to get the rest of the officers to move the class Halloween party to an old people's home. Big mistake!"

"I still think it was a good idea," Maris said, "treating people instead of tricking them. The old people would have really appreciated it. And the kids would have enjoyed it too if they would've just given it a try."

"Maris, I'm your friend—you know that. You can always count on me. But I've got to tell you: you just don't seem to get it! Kids just want to have fun. Why don't you try to loosen up a little bit?"

"I enjoy having fun as much as anyone," Maris said, "but I don't know why it's such a big deal to try to enjoy yourself while you're helping someone else. Serving others gives you a good feeling that you can't get any other way."

"Well, thank you, Pastor Hendricks, for that neat little sermon. I'm sure I'll be a better person for it!"

Maris's brown eyes flashed. "And thank you, Kristy, for the sarcasm. I thought friends were supposed to be supportive."

Kristy softened. "Hey, Maris, I'm sorry. You know I consider us best friends. But sometimes a friend has to kind of tell it like it is, you know what I mean? Sometimes a friend has to be the one to tell you bad news—to suggest a place here or there where you might consider making a change."

Maris sighed. "I know. I guess I'm more upset

about this election thing than I should be. I know it shouldn't be any big deal, but it really does hurt to be left out of something that you've been doing for so long. And it bothers me that kids at school don't seem to like me the way they used to."

Arriving at the parking lot in front of the school, they looked for their buses. Maris rode number 461 to Evanston Park; Kristy, number 316 to Belmont. Before she boarded her bus, Maris turned to her friend. "You still want to go to church with me tomorrow," she asked, "or have you changed your mind?"

Kristy grinned. "Yeah, I still want to go. I kind of enjoyed it last time. It isn't as boring as I thought it would be."

"I'll watch for you," Maris said.

On Sabbath morning Maris waited for Kristy on the front steps of the church. She arrived shortly before Sabbath school, and they headed for the youth room. "How you doing this morning?" Kristy asked. "Still stewing about the class elections yesterday?"

"Wish I could say I've forgotten about it completely," Maris said, "but it still bothers me that people object so much to things I've done. You'd think I was an ax murderer or something!"

"Oh, come on, Maris. It's only a class election. No one's said anything about an execution yet."

By now the youth pastor had tuned his guitar and had begun song service. As the program got under way, Maris offered up a silent prayer for God to help her try to forget the past week and concentrate on what was going on in Sabbath school.

The special feature was a married couple who

had just returned from a six-year mission assignment in the Amazon basin. They brought with them some objects that the people of the Amazon rain forest used in their everyday lives—a bowl made from a gourd, a blowgun, a beautifully crafted basket, and a short spear used to catch fish. Then they showed some color slides depicting the life of the people they had been working with. Maris was fascinated by the dramatic difference that could easily be seen in the people before and after they had accepted Christ into their lives. She could actually see Christ's love in their shining eyes.

Why can't you see such a difference between kids at school who are Christians and those who aren't? she wondered. *I don't think I look or act any different from anyone else, but everyone else—including Kristy—seems to think I do.*

Even so, the missionaries' experiences made her feel that someday she might consider going as a missionary to somewhere far away. She imagined herself teaching a large group of children under a tree, or maybe even treating sick people in a simple clinic in the jungle. By the time Sabbath school was over, she decided she would look into the possibilities someday. And maybe she'd consider going on the next short-term mission trip that the youth pastor organized during spring vacation each year.

It was then that she realized that Kristy had been unusually quiet. "What's the matter, Kris, something wrong?"

"Naw," Kristy said. "It's just that those missionaries have made me think about how you weren't elected to an office this week."

"Thanks for reminding me of that," Maris said, "but I don't see any connection."

"Well, it's just that this is the first time I've begun to see what you mean by helping others. Those missionaries gave up their good jobs and comfortable homes to go off to the wilds of the Amazon jungle to take Christianity to the people there. It's a cinch they didn't go there to have fun, what with all the bugs and snakes and stuff. Yet they talk as though they really found happiness in what they were doing out there in the hot, sticky jungle. That's kind of neat!"

"*You* can understand why people would go as missionaries to the Amazon?"

"What I mean is, now I think I can see a little better why you feel the way you do about helping others. It's a lot more important than winning a lousy class election."

Maris smiled. "I hadn't really thought it through like that."

"What's a friend for?" Kristy said.

"So," Maris asked, "does this change of heart mean you're thinking of becoming a missionary to Malaysia or Tanzania?"

"Well, as you know, geography isn't exactly my best subject," Kristy said with a grin. "Maybe—for now—we should just settle for the old people's home."

4 CLOUDY

Jessica came to us on a cold morning in April when the whole world was gray. Everything—the streets, the buildings, the sky—looked like a pencil drawing. Everything except her eyes. Jessica would have been just another ordinary-looking child had it not been for her eyes.

"Her father was killed in an automobile accident last week," the social worker had reported on the telephone. "And we can't seem to locate her mother. A neighbor said her mother lives back East somewhere, but he didn't know where. It may take us a little time to find her; can you take Jessica for us until then?"

Our home had long been a refuge for foster children. At times we had as many as four of them. Some stayed with us a week or two, others for as long as two years. Mom and Dad could never say no.

So when Mrs. Lange turned up on our porch that April morning, we took Jessica by the hand and led her into our lives, just as we had scores of others.

"Hello, dear," Mom said, kneeling down.

The little girl looked back at her with those dark, quiet eyes and said nothing.

"We're so happy to have you here with us," Mom coaxed. "This is Bill and Alex," she said, pointing to my brother and me.

"Hi, Jessica," I said, taking my cue. "We have a brand-new lamb out back. Would you like to come along with me to see it?"

Without a sound she took my hand, and I led her out to the field behind the house. When I caught the lamb and carried it to Jessica, the little girl threw her arms around the animal's neck and burst into tears.

I didn't know how to comfort her and stood awkwardly patting her on the head. "Jessica," I said, "is something wrong?" It was really a dumb question. How could anything be right for a 6-year-old who has only a government agency for parents?

She sobbed openly, huge, hot tears coursing down her cheeks. I knelt beside her and held the lamb as it struggled to get away from us. Finally, looking up at me with those eyes of hers, Jessica asked, "What's the lamb's name?"

"We don't have one for him yet. Would you like to name him? He can be your very own special friend, OK?"

She nodded, great gulping hiccups convulsing her little body. I brushed the hair off her perspiring forehead. "What would you like to name him?"

"Cloudy," she decided. "He looks just like a cloud up in heaven to me. That's where my daddy is."

"OK," I said, "we'll call the lamb Cloudy. That's a nice name."

Cloudy and Jessica became the closest of friends. Jessica took off after breakfast every morning, and the two of them frolicked through the fields of mustard for hours at a time. And slowly and quietly the lamb drew all the sadness out of the little girl. Jessica woke smiling in the morning and sang throughout the day.

As was our custom with all our foster children, we took Jessica to church with us. Religion was somewhat new to her; God was a name she had never heard before. She was amazed to discover that Christ was the same person mentioned in the word *Christmas.* She sat through Sabbath school in her little wooden chair, completely enrapt in everything she saw and heard. And then, all week long, she fired questions at us—the kind of questions that could occur only to children: "Where did God come from?" "Wasn't it awful 'yucky' for Jonah in the whale's tummy?" "Where is Noah's ark today?" "Does God love me too?"

It took only a short time for Sabbath school to become the highlight of the week for Jessica. She looked forward to it, sang its songs throughout the day, brightened with anticipation at the Sabbath morning breakfast table. She took to God as though He alone could take the place of the daddy she'd lost in an automobile accident. And her faith grew as big as the universe.

Several weeks after Jessica and Cloudy had become friends, we found the lamb one morning, lying on its side, unable to get up, and obviously sick. After Dad described the condition over the phone to the veterinarian, Dr. Kelvin said we would probably have to euthanize the animal. Some virus was making its rounds in the community. My dad, whose heart is as soft as a down pillow, picked the lamb up and carried it toward the barn.

"Where are you going with Cloudy?" Jessica asked.

Dad looked at her and said, "I'm sorry, Jessica, but Cloudy is a very sick little lamb. He's going to die, so I have to put him to sleep, or he may suffer."

Jessica grabbed the sleeve of Dad's jacket. "But Mr. Lawson," she said, "we could pray to God to make Cloudy well."

Dad went down on one knee. "Listen, Jessica, there's something you don't understand. Sometimes God doesn't bring healing. Sometimes it's better that He doesn't. You see, He knows best."

"Oh, Mr. Lawson," Jessica pleaded, "don't put Cloudy to sleep. If we pray to God about it, He will heal Cloudy."

Dad looked helplessly at each of us and took a deep breath. The life and death of lambs had always been a matter of course for us—a part of the natural process on a farm. It hadn't ever occurred to any of us before that we should ever interfere with it. God had far more important considerations.

But the child had him cornered. "All right, Jessica. We'll put Cloudy in the barn for a few days and see if he recovers. If he isn't better soon, though, I'll have to put him to sleep. It isn't right that we let the little fella suffer."

Jessica nodded eagerly, her big eyes shining. "God will make him well. I know He will."

We all followed Dad and Jessica out to the barn. Dad laid the lamb in a stall with some clean straw. Falling instantly to her knees, Jessica folded her hands and closed her eyes for a moment. Then she looked at us. "Aren't you going to pray for Cloudy with me?"

"Sure we are," I said, kneeling beside her. One by one, Dad, Mom, and Bill knelt too. And we prayed, each one of us, in our hearts, that if God ever did anything for a little girl, He'd do this for Jessica.

The next morning, Thursday, Jessica couldn't wait until breakfast was over to check on Cloudy. She ran excitedly out to the barn, and we followed, half expecting that surely God would step in and heal the lamb. But Cloudy was as sick as ever.

"Harold," Mother said, taking Dad's arm and pulling him aside. "You've got to do something for that animal. It's suffering so."

Dad nodded. "I know," he whispered, "but how can I take it away from Jessica? How will she ever understand?"

Meanwhile, Jessica's faith was concrete-firm. God hadn't healed Cloudy yet, but she knew He would, just as surely as He had the leper, the demoniac, the blind man—she knew every story and reminded us of every one.

"Let's give it one more day," Dad said privately to us as we watched Jessica play in the yard.

"If there's no change by tomorrow, I'll think of some way."

Friday morning was the same. Jessica raced out to the barn, with the rest of us trailing behind. But still the lamb showed no improvement.

"I've got an idea," Dad said to us back at the house. "I don't respect myself much for it, but I just don't know what else to do. Since we're going to Red Cloud this weekend to visit Uncle Bill and Aunt Lucille, I'll ask Mr. Chandler next door to come by the place and put Cloudy under. Maybe it'll be easier if Jessica isn't around when it happens."

Mother shrugged and took Dad's arm. "I know how you feel," she said. "A child's faith is such a fragile and beautiful thing. You hate to see anything happen to it."

So we packed ourselves up, including Jessica, and set out in the station wagon Friday afternoon for Red Cloud, 110 miles away. Dad's uncle and aunt lived there, an aging couple who had brought Dad up when his parents had passed away. Uncle Bill and Aunt Lucille were like grandparents to us.

"Will Cloudy be OK?" Jessica asked as we pulled out of the gravel driveway.

"God will do what is best for Cloudy," Mother said. Under her breath she muttered, "Now I know how Abraham felt when he said, 'God will provide.'"

Dad nodded and turned the station wagon onto Route 30.

The weekend was fantastic, as it always is at Uncle Bill and Aunt Lucille's. On Sabbath afternoon we drove out to the river for a picnic. That night we played games till bedtime. Just after lunch on Sunday we started for home. "Have you said anything to you-know-who?" Mother asked, nodding toward the back seat where Jessica sat watching the countryside roll by.

"No," Dad sighed. "I know I'm a coward. We'll just have to face the music when we get home."

The two-hour drive was a long, silent one for most of us. Jessica hummed tunes she had learned in Sabbath school, bounced back and forth between the front and back seats, and laughed and pointed out every white horse she could spot along the way. As happy as she was, it hurt to watch her.

But when we pulled up into the gravel driveway in front of the house, we instantly spotted Cloudy in the pen to the side of the barn, playing joyously and bleating almost arrogantly at us. We had never seen a healthier lamb.

While the rest of us gaped at Jessica as she played with the lamb, Dad headed for Mr. Chandler's to see what had happened. When he got back, all he could do was shrug. "Chandler says when he came over, he thought we must have made a mistake. The lamb looked fine to him, so he just let it be. Looks like the Lord truly does provide."

5 HASSLED HALF-PIPER

J.D. straightened up from lacing his boots and stood for a moment at the summit of Hopkins Knob just to savor the beauty of it all. Perfect! The sun was a huge, soft yellow circle in the low overcast sky, just above the ragged treetops. A few unusually large snowflakes drifted like dandelion down out of the gray overhead.

"Absolutely primo!" J.D. muttered to himself in wonder.

He snugged his worn Colorado Rockies baseball cap backward on his head and scanned the slope before him. At this time of the morning, he spotted only two or three skiers gliding down the hill. No problem with too many people on the slopes.

"Hey!" someone called from several feet behind him. "Sorry, but this run is supposed to be for skiers only. You'll have to take your snowboard over to Run Number 3. I think that's the only place they're allowed here."

"Who says?" J.D. snapped, turning to find a girl about his age sliding slowly toward him on skis. She wore a nifty coordinated ski outfit of white and fluorescent green with a matching pointed stocking cap. *Looks like a poster for some big-time ski resort like Killington or Squaw Valley,* he thought.

The girl smiled and shrugged. "Just the rules," she said, "for the safety of everyone. I was only trying to help—"

"Well, what happens if I just go ahead and shred this run anyway?"

The girl giggled. "Any number of things, I guess. You could get away with it. You could run into a skier and hurt the skier and yourself. I suppose you could even get thrown off the slopes—"

"And I could show these snobby skiers a thing or two about what to do with a perfectly good hill of snow! All they do is point their two planks toward the ski lodge and slither down the hill. Big deal! Isn't this supposed to be a free country?"

"Oh, yes," the girl agreed. "What was that our forefathers fought for? Life, liberty, and the pursuit of snowboarding?" Again she flashed a terrific smile, and J.D.'s rising anger melted instantly into a pool of slush. Suddenly he felt flustered and tongue-tied, as though he'd already spouted off way too much.

"Uh, well," he said at last, "I guess I'd better take a look at Run Number 3. I wouldn't want to get arrested or anything."

Again that smile. "Maybe I'll see you later,"

the girl said. She turned and set off down the slope toward the ski lodge.

From the moment J.D. first laid eyes on Run Number 3, however, he had to admit to himself that it wasn't half bad. Whoever designed and maintained it obviously knew something about what snowboarders were looking for in fun. It was what they call a "half-pipe," a groomed snow run about the length of a football field and the shape of a large bobsled track, with high vertical walls on each side.

"Absolutely primo!" he cried. With both boots strapped firmly to his yellow-and-black snowboard, J.D. "surfed" across the flatter bottom of the pipe as he built up speed and then hurtled directly up the curving right-hand wall, flying over the edge, twisting and turning in midair, before sliding back down the side. Then he crossed to the left side and repeated the same moves in reverse, this time performing a "fakie," riding the board backward across the middle of the pipe.

The rest of the day was a blur for J.D.—the absolute best he'd ever had on his board. He "carved up" that half-pipe. Each time he jumped back on the chair lift to return to the top of Hopkins Knob, he looked in every direction for the girl in green and white, but he couldn't see her anywhere. By 4:00, when he headed for the parking lot to catch a ride home with his aunt and uncle, he was almost beginning to wonder if he'd imagined her.

Thinking that a nice cup of hot chocolate might somehow ease his aching muscles a bit from all the bending and twisting exercise he'd been enjoying all day, he stopped by the ski lodge. Sauntering into the cafeteria with his snowboard under his arm, he headed for the food counter. But when he had to step aside to let a couple pass by, he tripped over a pair of ski boots that someone had left by a table. His board turned slightly and swept an entire dish pan of soapy water and dirty dishes and silverware off a small table, crashing it to the floor. Suddenly J.D. was the center of attention in a completely silent cafeteria. He quickly set his board against the wall and scrambled to clean up the mess.

A large, balding man in a white apron stormed through the door from the kitchen. "You 'shredheads' can't be happy endangering every skier on the slopes," he growled. "Now you're attacking us in the cafeteria!"

Then, appearing just as unexpectedly as she had at the top of the hill that morning, the girl with the terrific smile and the green-and-white ski outfit stepped in. "It's OK, Mr. Miller," she said. "This guy is a friend of mine. I'll help him clean things up. Here you go, 'Carve-Master,'" she said, handing a mop to J.D. "You mop up the water so no one slips and hurts himself, and I'll pick up what's left of these dishes."

It took several trips to the kitchen to wring out the mop before everything was completely cleaned up. Even though the crowd in the cafeteria had turned their attention elsewhere, J.D. decided to forget the hot chocolate after all and just get out of the place as quickly as possible. "Thanks," he said to the girl. "I guess you've kind of saved me twice today."

"No problem," she said.

"Uh, my name's J.D.," he said. "What's yours?"

"Kristen," she answered. "Kristen Hopkins."

In his confusion and embarrassment, it took a few moments for the significance of her name to sink in. "You mean *Hopkins,"* he said at last, "as in *Hopkins Knob?"*

"Yeah," she said. "My father kind of owns this place."

"You mean the lodge? the slopes? the hills? the trees? everything?"

"Yup."

"Well, no wonder you know where the snowboarders are supposed to be. I'm glad I took your advice this morning about the half-pipe on Run Number 3. If I'd gone ahead and done what I felt like doing at first, I'd have shredded Run Number 1 and someone would probably have made me leave."

"Probably true," she said.

"And I would never have learned your name," he added.

Later, when J.D. arrived at his uncle's car in the parking lot, there was something different about him that was immediately noticeable.

"What are you grinning about?" his uncle asked him.

J.D. whistled and shook his head. "It's been an interesting day," he said. "I've never been too clear before about what the Bible means by 'grace.' But after today, I know exactly what it's saying: *It's absolutely primo!"*

6 DO THE RIGHT THING

When Ciro and I pushed out through the thick glass doors of Tyler Mall, the August afternoon was waiting for us.

"Man, it's hot," Ciro groaned.

After spending an hour or two just kind of hanging out in the mall, we had checked out our usual places—The Gap, Waldenbooks, and The Wherehouse. In the meantime, we'd forgotten how hot it was getting outside. Now, with a new cassette in hand, we hurried to my black 4X4 in the parking lot. I jumped in and unlocked the door on Ciro's side. The engine roared to life, and I popped the cassette into the stereo. Great tunes! Holding his rolled-up copy of *Guitar* magazine in his hand like a microphone, Ciro shook back his black, shoulder-length hair and began to sing along. He has one of the worst singing voices I've ever heard, but that never has discouraged him.

We sat partway through the first song on the tape till the air-conditioning began to cool down the interior of the truck a bit. Then I shifted the 4X4 into reverse and began to back out of the parking space.

But something—the music or the heat or Ciro's sorry attempts at singing along—distracted me just enough that the front bumper of my truck caught the rear end of an old white Chevrolet Impala parked on my left. I felt the impact, saw the Impala next to me lurch slightly, and heard broken pieces of glass hit the pavement.

"Did you hit something?" Ciro asked, turning down the volume on the stereo.

I pounded the dashboard with my fist. "This is all I need!"

We jumped out and looked over the damage. My bumper was scratched on the underside a little—no big deal. But I had broken out the taillight of the Impala and dented some of its surrounding chrome.

"This is going to raise my insurance, and Dad will probably freak out," I fumed. "Why do things like this happen to me?"

"Bad break," Ciro said. He traced his finger along the dented chrome. "But who has to know? We can just split! Nobody's seen us. Life goes on!"

Though we're pretty good friends, in some ways Ciro and I are from different ends of the universe. Ever since I was a little kid, I've gone to church every week with my parents. Ciro hasn't ever seen the inside of a church. I've invited him to attend a youth meeting with me once in a while, but he usually just laughs and says no thanks.

Sometimes, from my point of view, it's hard to understand where he's coming from. I guess the thing that bothers me most about him is his lack of responsibility about some things. Not that I'm another Albert Schweitzer or anything like that. Ciro is always there for his friends, but for anyone else he's not overly concerned. He's the kind of guy who knows all those tacky jokes about starving Ethiopians. And he can be really kind of mean to people if he doesn't like them. I've never been comfortable with that.

We probably would have never hit it off at all if it hadn't been that when we were sophomores we got cut from the football tryouts for the Woodmont High School Raiders on the same day. He was too small and I was too slow. At the time I thought that the coach hadn't really given me a chance to show what I could do. I may give up a step or two against the really fast guys, but I have great hands. I was kind of spouting off about it in the cafeteria the next day when Ciro walked by.

"You got cut yesterday too?" he had asked, setting his tray down across from mine.

"Coach Walters always put me in against Kyle Anderson," I grumbled, "and who's going to do anything against an all-city safety? That guy covers pass receivers like a blanket."

Ciro shrugged and took a humongous bite out of his slice of pizza. "I weigh 145 pounds dripping wet, and the coach expects me to block a 200-pound lineman with arms like an octopus on steroids," he said. "But that's what the game is all about, I guess. Life goes on."

Now, two summers later, here I was, hearing Ciro say the same thing about a broken taillight in the Tyler Mall parking lot.

"Hey, look," I said. "I can't just drive away from this deal. It just isn't the right thing to do. I've got to leave my name and phone number on a slip of paper."

"Get real!" Ciro laughed. "How many times have you complained about people wrecking your paint job by banging their doors against your truck? Nobody's ever left a name and phone number for *you*. Besides, that car has to be 15 years old. It's got dents and scratches all over it. The driver probably won't even notice that you hit him."

I fingered a piece of the broken red taillight and thought about how long it would take me bagging groceries at Safeway to pay $100 worth of repairs on a 15-year-old heap. It suddenly seemed so needless and unfair. "Even if he does notice it," I muttered, "his insurance will cover it anyway. It won't cost him a cent."

Ciro looked at me and grinned. "Works for me!"

"Yeah," I said, "I guess you're right. Let's get out of here."

We jumped into the truck and headed for the exit to the parking lot. But as we sat waiting for the light to change at the first intersection, I got to thinking more about something Ciro had said: "How many times have you complained about people . . ." *What right*, I asked myself, *do I have to complain if I'm going to do the same thing to someone else? If I expect others to do the right thing, the least I can do is expect as much from myself. That's what the golden rule is all about.*

Ciro was just turning up the volume on the stereo again when I made a U-turn and headed back for the mall parking lot.

"What are you doing?" he asked.

"I'm going back," I sighed.

"Are you serious?"

"As a heart attack," I said.

Ciro ran his fingers through his hair. "Man, you are the weirdest guy I've ever known. Nobody in his right mind would do what you're doing. You were home free, and now you're going back."

"I may have been home," I said, "but I wouldn't have been free."

Ciro blinked and looked at me as if I'd begun to speak Russian or something. He turned away and watched the traffic, seemingly lost in thought for the moment.

"A hundred dollars, maybe more," he finally blurted out. "That's what this doing the right thing is going to cost you!"

"You know," I said, "a wise man once told me something that makes pretty good sense: 'Life goes on.'"

He laughed and shook his head. "Words to live by!"

By now we were back at the "scene of the crime." I scrawled out my name and phone number on the receipt from The Wherehouse and slipped it under the windshield wiper of the Impala.

When I got back into the truck, Ciro looked at me a long moment. "Maybe I can lend you a little to help you out for a while," he said.

I smiled. "You'll be hearing from me," I said.

7 STARTING OVER

The last three miles from the county road to the cabin were a twisting route—two dusty ruts and something less. Where the way dipped into a dry creek bed, there were only rocks and sand.

Jeff lurched irritably in the seat as Dad swung the steering wheel to avoid granite boulders. "Only another mile and a half," his father said brightly, but Jeff said nothing.

He was thinking of Mom at home, and he wished he were there. "Why do I have to go, Mom?" he'd asked.

"Your father doesn't get to see you much since we've been separated," Mom had said. "You know that. He's taking a full week off during your vacation to do something special for you."

"Well, I wish he wouldn't bother," Jeff had

interrupted. "He never cared enough about us before to stay home and take care of us."

Dad screeched the jeep to a stop in front of a cabin, dust following them like a plague. Jeff fanned his face with his hand. "Is this it?"

"This is it!" Dad said. "How come you've been so quiet? I thought you'd really enjoy the ride in from the road."

"It was all right," Jeff mumbled, leaping out of the jeep to avoid looking directly into Dad's eyes. "Come on. I guess we'd better get this stuff into the cabin."

Dad sat behind the wheel for a few moments and watched as Jeff tried to look busy.

"Jeff," Dad said, "I'd like to say something right up front. I know I've hurt you and your mother many times, but—"

"I'd really rather not talk about it right now," Jeff interrupted.

Dad hesitated for a moment, then he grabbed his sleeping bag from the back of the jeep and headed for the cabin. By the time supper was over and the dishes were put away, the evening was getting late.

"Well," Dad said as he hung the dish towel on the rack, "what do you want to do now? Shall we go down to the lake for a while?"

"I'm kind of tired, Dad. I think I'll turn in now."

Dad looked a little disappointed. "OK, son. Maybe tomorrow."

Jeff rolled his sleeping bag out on the upper bunk. He could feel Dad's eyes on him, and he knew Dad felt bad. But he crawled into the bag and rolled over, facing the wall.

◀ ▶

The room was beginning to lighten, the furniture taking shape in the early morning, when Jeff rolled over and opened his eyes. His father was hunkered down before the stone fireplace, touching a hissing match to the crumpled newspaper under a small stack of kindling.

For a few minutes Jeff quietly watched his father. The memory of the bitter fights between Mom and Dad returned for the thousandth time. Dad's drinking problem and Mom's frustration had finally split them up. Jeff bit his lip and wondered if there was any real hope of Dad's coming home. As he watched his father, he suddenly wanted to say something, but he was afraid to.

Dad stared silently into the newborn fire as it grew before him. Then he turned and caught Jeff looking at him. "Morning!" he said.

"Hi," Jeff said.

"What do you want to do today? We can just relax around the cabin, go boating out on the lake, climb Big Eagle Rock—"

Jeff stretched. "Let's climb, I guess."

While he straightened up his sleeping bag, got dressed, and washed his face, Dad fried some pretty good pancakes for breakfast. Jeff mentioned this, and Dad seemed very pleased.

After breakfast they filled canteens, put on climbing boots, and headed for Big Eagle Rock. The morning was still cool, with the first rays of the sun just touching the tops of the trees. The going was easy for the first hour, the trail leading through the forest, its ground almost spongy with the rich humus carpet. Jeff led the way, not looking back at Dad, and saying little.

When they reached the base of Big Eagle Rock, Jeff sat down under a poplar to rest a while. Big Eagle Rock was a huge dome, round at the base and, on the top, flat as an overturned cereal bowl. Jeff shaded his eyes and squinted at the top of it. "Doesn't look very challenging to me."

"Oh, it isn't really. I had to promise your mother we wouldn't do anything foolish, or she'd never have let me bring you up here. It isn't dangerous, but I think you'll get a kick out of the climb. Let's give it a try."

Dad led Jeff to a six-foot-wide split in the rock that led diagonally up toward the summit in almost step-like zigzags. "You go first," Dad said, "and I'll follow you up."

Jeff grabbed a rock outcropping and pulled himself upward. The climb was not as easy as it looked, but there was always a place for a foothold. Within 15 minutes he was ready for a breather. He stopped and looked back down over his shoulder. "Want to rest a minute?" he asked.

"Sure," Dad said.

Jeff shouldered into a sort of corner in the rock, but just as he was beginning to feel secure, a small piece gave way beneath his left foot, and he began to slide on his back toward his father.

Quickly Dad pinned him to the rock so he could grab hold, but in so doing, his father lost his grasp and tumbled down the incline to the bottom of the dome, his arms and legs swinging wildly like a doll thrown by a careless child.

"Dad!" Jeff yelled. "Are you all right?"

His father moved slightly and seemed to mumble something Jeff couldn't quite hear. As quickly and carefully as he could, Jeff scrambled to his father's side. By the time he got there, Dad had sat up. He smiled—or tried to—and his eyes looked glazed. "It's my leg," Dad hissed through gritted teeth.

Jeff pulled up Dad's pantleg. Blood oozed from a wound above the ankle, and a jagged piece of yellow bone stuck out. Jeff blinked and fought back a wave of nausea.

"What'll we do, Dad? You can't walk, and I can't carry you!"

Dad closed his eyes and swept in a deep breath.

What if he dies? Jeff thought. Realizing he was on the verge of panic, he fought to think quickly but clearly. "What can I do?" he moaned in frustration. Then he thought of the ranger station four miles from the cabin. They had passed it in the jeep only the day before. "I'll go to the ranger station for help," he said. "Will you be OK here alone?"

Dad nodded.

Without another word Jeff launched himself toward the cabin. Because the lake was in the way, he would have to take the trail to the cabin and then follow the dirt road from there to the ranger station at Manzanita Flat. When he arrived at the cabin, he stopped and looked for a moment at the jeep. With driver's education still several months away, the jeep was useless to him. He turned and headed down the road. "Four miles to go," he muttered.

Within minutes his lungs were bursting and his legs felt like sandbags. Jeff slowed to a fast walk, but he kept going. Then, when he'd caught his breath, he broke into a run again. Finally he spotted the ranger station through the trees and sprinted with new energy.

The ranger station was deserted. The garage door stood open, but the cabin was locked up tight.

Jeff ran around the cabin twice, rattling the doors, peering in the windows. No one was there. On the wall in the kitchen he saw a telephone, but it might as well have been on another continent. Desperately he ran again to the front door. Hunching his shoulder, he piled into the door with all his might, but the door held its ground.

Cold sweat prickled at his neck and back, and his stomach hollowed. *What can I do?* he wondered. He decided to try the back door again.

Scrambling down the steps of the front porch, he tripped over a large stone placed as decoration along the walkway to the road. He kicked at the stone in frustration and then suddenly realized he'd found a way to get into the ranger station. With difficulty he managed to lift the stone and lug it to the kitchen window. Without hesitation he used his own momentum to heave the stone through the window. Then, taking care that he didn't cut himself on the jagged frame, he crawled through the window to the telephone.

When the operator came on, Jeff blurted out his problem. The operator called another ranger station. "Return to where your father is," the operator said. "The ranger will meet you there."

When Jeff arrived back at the base of Big Eagle Rock, his father lay completely still. Fearfully, Jeff shook Dad's shoulder, and Dad groaned and opened his eyes.

"Help is on the way, Dad. I phoned from the ranger station."

Dad shook his head but said nothing. Finally his mind seemed to clear. "Jeff," he said, putting his hand on his son's shoulder, "I'll be all right."

Jeff looked at Dad's ashen face, the thin, grim line of his mouth, the almost childlike pain in his face. He thought of how hard Dad was trying to be a father to him again this week, and of the selflessness Dad had shown in risking his own safety to protect him. He had thought that Dad didn't care about him or Mom, but maybe he had begun to change.

Jeff touched his father's hand. "Dad," he said, "do you think we could try being a family again?"

Dad nodded feebly and smiled. "I'm really glad to hear you say that. I've been trying to find a way to tell you that I've quit drinking. We'll talk to your mother about starting over."

8 GIVE AND TAKE

The flow of shoppers in Sunrise Mall was like rush hour on the freeway as Sue and Tina walked out of Waldenbooks.

"When the stores all decide to have a sale at the same time," Tina joked, "people come out of the woodwork. Just one more stop for us, and we can head out to meet my brother Kevin at the car."

A couple of stores down the mall from Waldenbooks, the two girls stopped to look at some sweaters on the table in front of The Gap. Now nearly through their sophomore year of high school, they had been friends since sixth grade.

Sue nudged Tina as she held up a yellow sweater in front of her. "You really wanted that copy of *Seventeen,* didn't you?"

Tina smiled. "Yeah. I was interested in that

article about how you can dress like a million without going broke."

"How bad did you want the magazine?" Sue asked with just a touch of mischief in her voice.

"Well, it doesn't really matter," Tina sighed. "I have only enough money to buy that CD Kevin wants for his birthday. Maybe by the end of the month I'll come back in and get that issue of *Seventeen* before they take it off the shelf."

"No problem," Sue said. "Look what I've got!" She slipped a brand-new copy of the magazine out of her jacket. "Here." She offered the magazine to Tina. "A little gift to my best friend."

Tina blinked. "I thought you said you didn't have any money."

"I don't," Sue said with a shrug.

Suddenly Tina felt a little sick. "Sue, did you just take that magazine without paying for it?"

Sue giggled. "Just wanted to see if I could get away with it."

"I can't believe you did that, Sue. You know it isn't right to take stuff that doesn't belong to you. A 6-year-old knows that much."

"Get real," Sue said, her voice rising. "So I swiped a measly $2 magazine! It isn't like I held the place up. You're acting like I'm a terrorist or something. I haven't hurt anybody."

Tina looked a long moment at Sue. She knew that Sue's feelings were hurt, but she was also a bit hurt herself, considering that Sue would expect her to accept a gift that had been stolen—even if they were best friends.

"Look, Sue, I'm really sorry, but I just don't feel good about this."

Sue's eyes flashed. "Now I suppose you think I should go back into the store and return the magazine and apologize," she snapped. "Well, I'm not going to do it. I really don't see why you're making such a big deal out of this. I thought we were friends."

"We were—still are—friends, Sue. That's why I can't let you do this. I care about you."

Sue looked down at her feet. "Well, if you don't want the magazine, I guess that's your business," she said. "Maybe it wasn't the best thing to do, but I'm not going to take it back. Even if I were willing to do that, I don't have any money with me."

"Well, I do," Tina said. "I'll be right back." Without giving Sue a chance to say anything, Tina left her standing in the middle of the mall and walked back into the bookstore. The clerk behind the counter had to wait on two other customers before he could turn his attention to Tina, and three others had lined up behind her in the meantime. Twice she very nearly gave up on her idea and considered leaving the store.

"May I help you?" the clerk finally asked.

Tina gulped. "A friend of mine took a copy of a magazine from your store a while ago, and I'd like to pay you for it now," she said.

The man smirked. "A friend?" he asked, looking around the store.

Tina flushed. She knew he suspected that she herself had taken the magazine and had returned because her conscience was bothering her. "Yes," she said, "it was a copy of *Seventeen,* and I believe it was $2, plus whatever tax there is." She laid three $1 bills on the counter, received her change, and quickly walked out of the store without looking back.

Sue was still standing in the very same place Tina had left her. She looked up when Tina returned. "What did you do?" Sue asked.

"I paid for the magazine," Tina said. "Now we can go."

"But now you won't have enough for Kevin's CD," Sue protested.

"Not today," Tina said, "but I can come back later in the week after I get my money for baby-sitting the Silva kids. Mrs. Silva said she'd probably be able to pay me on Tuesday."

"I don't get it," Sue said. "Why did you go back and pay for the magazine?"

"I don't know, exactly," Tina said. "I guess the least I can do is spare a couple of dollars to help a friend who's made a mistake."

As Sue and Tina walked out the large glass doors of the mall, Sue was silent. The temperature had dropped and a fine white dusting of snow was just beginning to accumulate on the ground. They got into Kevin's empty car in the parking lot; it would be at least another 15 minutes before he would meet them to take them home.

At last Sue broke the silence. "I said I hadn't hurt anybody, but I hurt you and I hurt myself. Thanks for being the kind of friend you are."

Tina reached over and gave Sue's hand a squeeze. "Do me a favor," she said. "Read me that article on how I can dress like a million without going broke!"

9 GRACE

Grace stood with her hands on her hips. Humming "Swing Low, Sweet Chariot," she looked at the open suitcase before her and wondered what to take.

"We're going on an eight-week tour," Lionel had said. "We'd like you to come along. You can sing backup and maybe even a solo or two once you get into the swing of it. How about it?"

That had been two weeks ago, and Grace still grinned like a child at the thought of it. Finally, she was going to get her chance to leave town. To be in a different city every night, singing for audiences across the country—and getting paid for it! She folded a pair of blue jeans and laid them in the suitcase.

Soon she was ready to go, and it was time to tell her mother she was leaving. Grace had been watching for a strategic time to do this, but always she had put it off. Tonight it had to be done. Taking a deep breath, she headed for the living room. Her rehearsal of this announcement had never come out right. She knew how it would end. For her mother there was only gospel music.

Grace sat down on the couch next to her mother, who was engrossed in a *Guideposts* article. For a moment she only looked at her, at the unruly, silvering hair and the full mouth that quivered slightly as she read—at her mother's hands.

"Mama," Grace half whispered. Her mother made no move, no sign of having heard her. She continued to read, seemingly oblivious to her daughter's presence. *She's just playing possum,* Grace mused. *She always knows when something's up anyway.*

"Mama," Grace repeated, "I know you hear me, and I need to talk to you."

With unnecessary deliberation, her mother laid the magazine down in her lap, removed her rimless glasses, and looked at Grace. She still said nothing.

"Mama, I'm leaving tomorrow on a singing tour. I've been offered a real good job." Grace instantly regretted the abrupt way she was announcing this.

Finally her mother broke her silence. "Where are you going?"

"Clear across country," Grace brightened, "to Chicago, Cincinnati, Pittsburgh, Washington, D.C. I'm so excited!"

"You going to sing gospel music?"

Grace looked at the floor. "No. I'll be going with Lionel Green and his group."

Her mother frowned.

"Mama, I'll be able to make real good money, and I can buy you some nice things for a change."

"Don't you be putting this on me," her mother flared. "I've got everything I need. If you take this job, it's because you want to go, not because you need to buy me anything."

There was a long moment of hissing silence during which Grace's mother muttered, "Don't need to buy me nothin'!" She reiterated this several times, but she somehow seemed to be crumbling, until finally she looked at Grace with huge tears in her eyes and lips quivering. "Grace, what you do with your life is between God and you. But don't use me as an excuse for leaving. I have everything I want out of this world. I'm not unhappy."

Things would have been easier for Grace if her mother had become angry and ranted and raved about her leaving. Then she could have stalked out of the house and felt pretty good about it. But something in her mother's quiet, almost childlike acquiescence cut deeply into Grace's feelings. She clenched her jaw. "I'm going, Mama. I want to be a singer, and I don't have to give up what I believe to do that. You'll see. I'll make you proud."

Her mother said nothing more, only sat silently shaking her head, her arms folded, and her tear-filled eyes fixed on the wall opposite her. Grace sat for a long time there in the living room with her mother. She wanted to say more, to explain the deep desires within her, but her mother was living in the days of Moses and the Israelites. She would never understand.

With a heavy sigh, Grace stood up. There was nothing more to do than go to bed. Plans for the concert tour swam around inside her. *Sure*, she thought, *it'll be hard on Mama at first, and I'll miss her too. But in the long run, when I've really made a success of myself, she'll see I made the right decision.*

Images of herself onstage in blue-white light came up before her, of thousands of fans swaying and clapping to the rhythm of her music, of guitars and piano and drums pounding out the pulsing life of the music. And she, Grace Garrett, would be at the center of all that excitement.

She sat wearily down on her bed and looked at her image in the mirror over the vanity table. People said Grace looked exactly like her mother had as a young girl—the same large brown eyes, the same full mouth. Her mother, too, had a good singing voice. One of Grace's warmest memories was of singing next to her mother in the church choir. Music for them both was the most meaningful part of worship.

Grace looked at the picture of her mother on the dresser. A small newspaper clipping filled the corner of the frame: "Woman saves daughter from fire." Memory seared her. Mama's hands and arms still carried the scars.

Tears suddenly filled Grace's eyes, and for a time she wept in sheer desperation.

She lay awake most of the night, listening to the silent battle going on in her head. The last time she had looked at the clock it was 3:00 a.m., but she woke at the sound of her mother clattering a pot on the stove in the kitchen. The morning was cool, and the first orange glow of the new sun filled the window.

She shuffled sleepily into the kitchen. "What's for breakfast, Mama?" Her mother was deftly cracking eggs one-handed, letting them plop into a pan. Grace noticed with a wry smile the same yellow-flowered housecoat and floppy felt slippers her mother had worn for years it seemed.

"How do eggs sound?" her mother asked without looking up. It wasn't a question to be answered. It was routine, Mama's way of announcing the breakfast fare. Slipping two slices of bread into the toaster, her mother asked, just as casually, "When do you have to leave?"

Grace sighed as she looked out the kitchen window. "I'm not going."

Mama looked at Grace for the first time that morning. She started to speak and then thought better of it. Returning to the sizzling eggs, she said, "Breakfast will be ready in a minute."

10 UNCLE HARRY'S POSTCARD FROM HEAVEN

When I was 8 years old, our mailman was family. "Postal workers," they call them today to be politically correct. And sometimes you hear of one of them going berserk with a semiautomatic weapon in a fast-food restaurant. But I lived my childhood in a gentler time; ours was a mailman.

About 2:00 every afternoon—except on Sunday, of course—he lurched around the corner of Bel Canto Drive with three or four children trailing happily along behind him. The sweat of a hot summer afternoon seeped through the back of his blue-gray shirt and the band of his cap, and ran in slick rivulets down the back of his neck.

"Hello, Mrs. Swanson," he'd say, handing Mom a fistful of mail. "I see your aunt from Stockton is here for the weekend." (He always recognized her car parked in the driveway.) "Say hello to her for me, will you?"

Every kid on the block called him Uncle Harry. He was as much a part of Bel Canto Drive as the English walnut trees along the street. It was as if the developers of our neighborhood of tract houses had designed the development to include him. The sight of his leather mail sack and crooked walk, with one shoulder hunched up to carry the extra weight of the mail, brought us bounding over hedges and across lawns to call out, "Hi, Uncle Harry!"

He'd grin and say, "How you doin' there, Sport!" with a fascinating twitch in his left eye and a sweep of his hand across his forehead.

On Saturdays he'd usually arrive during dinner and would allow himself to be coaxed into the house for a glass of ice water and a few minutes' chat. He'd ask how the lawn was coming in the backyard and how Great-grandma Davis was feeling lately.

Uncle Harry threatened to retire just about every summer, when only the grasshoppers and 10-year-old street softball enthusiasts ventured out into the heat. The grasshoppers sailed along three or four inches over the ground, making a sound like gritting teeth. Uncle Harry would watch one of the creepy insects with oversized eyes light on the smooth bark of a walnut tree and talk of hanging up his mailbag for good.

"One of these days," he'd say, "I'm going to take a nice long trip to Hawaii, and I'm going to just sit on a beach in my shorts and drink massive quantities of pineapple juice all day." Then he'd snuff and rub his nose with the back of his hand and continue on his route down Bel Canto. He probably had a huge territory to cover, but we kids considered Uncle Harry our own private mailman.

Then one day a new postal worker came around the palm tree at the corner. The softball that my brother Kenny had just hit dropped, untouched, and rolled up against the curb as we gaped at the new mailman.

He marched up the street with a confident, almost military, stride, sorting mail as he went and tucking it with dispatch into the proper boxes along the way. He probably didn't even know we were there until my question seemed to awaken him, as if from a trance.

"Where's Uncle Harry?"

"Who?" he asked. He had the look of someone afraid of becoming the butt of a practical joke. His protruding Adam's apple bobbed up and down nervously.

"Uncle Harry," Kenny repeated, "our mailman."

"Oh, Harry Englewood retired last Friday," he replied.

It was the first time any of us had ever considered that Uncle Harry would have a last name.

"Are you our new mailman?" Kenny asked.

"Welcome to life, kid," he said with a nod. Then he stepped off, as if on some silent command, and continued his new assignment down the street. We watched him grow smaller and smaller as he reached the other end and disappeared around the corner. He wasn't anything like Uncle Harry, and we instantly resented the effrontery of the post office department for thinking this impostor would ever be able to carry Uncle Harry's mail sack on Bel Canto Drive.

Six-year-old Kenny looked at me and blinked. "Where do people go when they retire? Do you think Uncle Harry's gone to heaven?" It was exactly the kind of thing Kenny often asked.

"Naw," I said. "Probably just Hawaii."

Sure enough, a couple weeks later we got a postcard picturing palm trees and Diamond Head at sunset. It was from Uncle Harry. "Aloha to the Swanson family" it read on the back in broad, scratchy lettering. "Say hello from Uncle Harry to all the kids on Bel Canto Drive. At last I've made it to heaven!" It was a comment that stirred up my theology for several months—and Kenny's even longer.

I guess that was the first time in my life I'd ever considered a world—and a time—larger than Bel Canto Drive. I didn't like the feeling at first, but the more I thought about people like Uncle Harry being in heaven, the better heaven sounded to me.

11 EVERYDAY EMBARRASSMENTS

Already at least 15 minutes late, I hurried past the usual couple panhandlers, slipped my magnetic fare card into the slot, and pushed through the turnstile of the Silver Spring Metro Station. Even the escalators seem slow when you're in a hurry. When the train finally rolled to a stop at the platform, I found a seat next to a window and opened my copy of *Sports Illustrated*. With my destination now 14 stops and 45 minutes away, I had some time for a little reading.

I was halfway through an article when a crackly voice hissed "Fort Totten" over the intercom as the Metro slowed into the next station. It drew to an abrupt stop and the doors rolled open, allowing a fresh supply of morning commuters to pour in.

Among the secretaries and college students and shoe store salespeople and bank tellers, a boy of about 12 carefully picked his way through the bigger, heedless bodies, trying to find a place for himself. Wearing a Baltimore Orioles baseball cap, sweatshirt, jeans, and hopelessly worn-out Nikes, he carried in his hands a rectangular piece of cardboard, with a clumsily made structure on it. Undoubtedly a school project of some kind. The boy sidled into the seat in front of me, trying to protect with his own small body the odd thing he was carrying, as though he was afraid it might be crushed in the flow of humanity. Setting it down between himself and the window, he half leaned forward, seemingly trying to keep others from seeing it.

I'm usually like the other thousands of commuters on the Metro; I seldom speak a word to anyone around me. But something about the boy piqued my interest. Leaning toward him, I asked, "What do you have there, a school project of some kind?"

The boy nodded but said nothing.

"What is it," I asked, "the Alamo?"

"No," he said quietly.

"I know," I said, "it's the White House, where the president lives."

"Nope," the boy said.

"Hey," I said with a smile, "if you don't want to tell me what it is, you don't have to. But I really am interested. I'm not just trying to give you a hard time."

The boy looked at me and then at the other passengers around us. No one else was paying any attention to either of us, so he decided to answer. "It's a tomb."

"A tomb?" I asked. "Whose tomb is it?"

"It's the tomb of Jesus."

"What's it for?" I asked.

"Mrs. Turner, our teacher, assigned us to make some kind of special project about an important event in history. The rest of the kids are building models of a printing press, the Battle of Waterloo, the Pilgrims landing on Plymouth Rock—stuff like that."

"Where do you go to school?"

"Kennedy Elementary, over on Forest Glen Road."

"You must be a Christian."

"Yeah," he said simply.

"Tell me," I couldn't help asking, "some of the other kids in your class are probably not Christians. What do you think they'll say about your project? Think they'll see the historical importance of Jesus?"

The boy shrugged. "Yeah, right! Most of them don't ever go to church. About all they know is that Christmas is supposed to be Jesus' birthday."

I nodded. "I guess that's the way it is for us Christians in this world, isn't it? How do you feel about that? Do the kids in school sometimes make fun of you?"

The boy was silent for a long moment. He looked out the window of the train at the trees and homes whooshing by. Finally he nodded. "The other day someone asked me if I had seen something on TV on Sunday morning. Lester Johnson butted in, 'No, Darnelle goes to church on Sunday mornings. He's a Jesus boy!'" Tears came to his eyes. He bit his lip and tried to avoid it, but the impact of the incident had left a small wound that had not yet healed. He looked away from me again—to avoid my eyes.

"It's OK, Darnelle," I said. "I think I know how you feel. I've had people say the same kinds of things about me at times in my life."

"You know," he said, "it really makes me feel ashamed."

"Hey," I said, "don't be ashamed of being a Christian—ever. I know it hurts sometimes, but just try to keep Paul and Peter and Stephen and the other apostles in mind. They had to put up with the same thing. Isn't it kind of neat to know we face some of the same challenges that guys like that did?"

The boy shook his head. "That's not what I mean. I'm not ashamed of being a Christian. What I'm ashamed of is that I let the kids at school embarrass me all the time."

"Forest Glen," the intercom crackled again.

"Whoa," Darnelle said, "this is where I get off. Gotta go!"

He gathered up his class project, exited through the open doors and was gone.

Half an hour later, when my own station came along, I rolled up my copy of *Sports Illustrated* and headed for the exit. Just outside the turnstiles an old man fell in step beside me, reached out tentatively and touched the sleeve of my jacket. "Hey, kid," he said, "can you spare some change?"

My first instinct was to say nothing and keep on walking. I'd done that very thing a hundred times before. If you don't make eye contact, the embarrassment doesn't have to last all that long. Another pace or two and he would have gotten the message.

But then I remembered the boy on the train with the class project. If he could face the embarrassment of sharing Jesus' tomb with a bunch of kids who think Plymouth Rock was a big deal, the least I could do was buy breakfast for some homeless guy.

12 HOOPING IT UP!

Coach Robinson glanced at the diagram on his clipboard one more time, loosened his tie, and leaned into the huddle around the players' bench. He could hardly make himself heard above the crowd as the band started to play the school song.

Turning his back to the other team's bench, Coach cupped his hands around his mouth. "All right, guys, lean in here close," he shouted. "Fourteen seconds to go, and we're two points down. I don't think we have time for two baskets, and we can't count on the other team to foul us. We'll have to go for the three-pointer. Taylor, you get the ball in bounds to Stevens. Leigh, as soon as the ball is passed in bounds, set a pick on the right side for Webster. Stevens, as soon as you see Web open, get the ball to him. Web, you'll have only one chance. Don't pass it and don't hesitate; just go immediately up for the shot. It has to be a three-pointer. Any questions?"

The five players on Camden High's basketball team looked around at one another. They had practiced this last-minute play countless times in drills; they all knew there was no need for questions now. Mitch Stevens, the point guard and captain of the team, looked up at the clock and grimaced. He ran a hand across his forehead.

"Let's just do it!" he shouted.

With a yell, the Camden Cougars, in their sweat-soaked purple and gold uniforms, leaped to their feet and took their places out on the gym floor.

Fourteen seconds. Cory Webster raked his fingers through his hair. He had no time to be nervous. The Cougars had to win this game against Stockton High to get into the playoffs. As the Cougars' leading scorer, he knew the team would be counting on him at a time like this. In a way he was used to pressure situations. He also knew that—win or lose—the team would support him. They were a good bunch of guys.

Cory saw Marcus Leigh take his position near the top of the key, and then he quickly looked away. He didn't want to give the other team any hint that Leigh would be setting a pick for him.

The referee blew his whistle and tossed the ball to Taylor along the sideline in front of the opponents' bench. For a moment the gym became as silent as a cave, except for the *chirp* of basketball shoes and the *thump, thump* of the basketball on the glistening wooden floor. The opposing center, the tallest player on the court, barked something about watching the top of the key. Taylor faked a pass to Lydell and snapped the ball to Stevens, who quickly dribbled up the left side of the court. The opposing guard—in red and white—took a swipe at the ball in an attempt to steal it, but Stevens deftly turned to protect it, placing his body between the ball and the guard. Just as Stevens crossed the midline, Cory brushed past Leigh on the right, just the way they'd practiced it, looked toward Stevens, and saw the ball already sailing directly at him. With one smooth motion, Cory caught the ball chest-high, pivoted on his left foot, leaped, and pumped the ball in a steep arc for the basket. The buzzer sounded, the ball swished cleanly through the net, and the Camden High School gymnasium erupted in a thunderous wave of noise.

Cory thrust his fists triumphantly into the air and was instantly swarmed by his teammates. Shouting and laughing and rolling around on the floor, the players, as well as dozens of their classmates from the bleachers, hugged one another and howled. Unbelievable! They had upset Stockton High and were going to go to the playoffs! Cheerleaders and their classmates were hugging one another, some of them in tears. Even in all the confusion, Cory remembered to breathe a silent prayer of thanks.

With the band playing "We Are the Champions," Cory scrambled to his feet and headed for the locker room. He shook the hand of a Stockton High player in red and white, who mumbled something about seeing him again in the playoffs. Then Coach Robinson clapped him on the shoulder.

"Beautiful shot, Web," he said with a big grin. "Worked just like the diagram on my clipboard!"

Cory smiled and looked down at his feet. "Well, Coach, it did this time, anyway."

He picked his way through the crowd and pushed through the locker room door. Players pounded their fists exultantly on the lockers, stood on the benches, and howled like wolves. Cory sat heavily down on the wooden bench next to his locker, peeled off his jersey, and wiped the perspiration off his face and neck with it. Suddenly he felt very tired. Even now it was hard to believe that they'd beaten Stockton High. He shook his head in disbelief.

Mitch Stevens flopped down next to him and gave him a high-five. "If you *never* make another shot in your life," he said, "you'll always have that one to brag about!"

Cory shook his head. "You had that pass right on the money, Mitch. I looked up and there it was. You just passed it where you knew I'd be. Couldn't have asked for anything more. Everything just fell into place for us today. I can't take much credit for it."

Mitch looked silently at Cory for a moment. The steam from the shower room was already billowing out into the locker area, and Mitch stood up and headed for the showers. "Where's Lydell?" he shouted.

For more than an hour, the players' shouts echoed throughout the locker room. Coach Robinson had gone into his office and was talking on the telephone. Someone in the next bank of lockers had turned on a portable radio, its tinny music sounding thin and far away. The locker room manager was complaining about somebody leaving his towels on the floor.

After his shower, Cory had dressed in his Levis and fluorescent green Nike T-shirt. He was just slicking back his wet hair with a comb when Mitch moved in next to him in front of the mirror. Wearing a black Chicago Bulls cap backward on his head, Mitch gave Cory a nudge in the ribs and glanced toward Coach Robinson's office.

"The whole team's going to Taylor's house tonight," he said. "We are going to party big time, dude! You can make it, can't you?"

Cory ran his thumbnail slowly over the teeth of his comb and hesitated. He knew his teammates could get pretty rowdy at times. From things they'd said in the locker room and on the team bus, the parties they went to weren't at all like those he was used to with his youth group at church. When he was with the youth group, he didn't have to worry as much about being tempted to do something he knew wasn't right. He could be comfortable. And none of his teammates, as far as he knew, had ever seen the inside of a church.

"I don't know, Mitch. I was thinking—"

"Come on, Web," Mitch coaxed. "We're not going to do anything to make you lose your religion. Lighten up a little! You've got to be there after a game like this one. You're the big hero."

Cory looked again at Mitch. He was the one who had first nicknamed him Web. Now the whole team—even Coach Robinson—called him that. Cory smiled. "I guess I can come by for a while."

"All right!" Mitch said. "Hey, and may I catch

a ride to Taylor's with you in your car?"

"Sure," Cory said, slipping on his Oakleys. "Let's go."

The drive to Kenny Taylor's house was across town, and traffic held them up a bit. Mitch and Cory talked about the game and about what they were planning to do for spring vacation.

"I guess I'll probably spend the whole week working at Baskin-Robbins," Cory said. "I need the money for a couple new tires."

Mitch looked at Cory. "Hey, Web, back there in the locker room you said that you couldn't take much credit for winning the game today. You're the hero of the game. What do you mean you can't take credit for it?"

Cory thought for a minute. "Well," he said, "I have worked hard during practice to improve my basketball skills. But I believe that God is the one who gave me my talent for basketball, and I can't take credit for that. We're all born with God-given talents of one kind or another. Some people are naturally good at math or art or sports or science, but how can they take credit for something they were born with?"

"Don't let Coach Robinson hear you talking like that," Mitch said with a grin. "He will be telling everybody for months about how you won tonight's game because of his clipboard diagram!" Mitch slipped into a poor imitation of Coach Robinson's voice: "Men, the three most important elements of basketball are execution, execution, execution!"

Cory smiled. "Yeah, I know," he said. "But the fact is, there are all kinds of things that came together for us in this game. Coach's diagrams, our hard work in practice, your perfect pass from mid-court, and my jump shot. But I believe it is God who gives us the abilities to do those things—win or lose."

"Is that why you spend so much time with your church youth group instead of partying with us?" Mitch asked. "Seems like you're always going somewhere or doing something with them."

"Partly," Cory said. "But I also do a lot of stuff with them just because we can help one another to get to know God better."

Mitch gazed a bit absently at the houses going by. "What kinds of stuff do you do in your church youth group?" he asked.

"All kinds of things," Cory said. "We go on picnics, play games, visit the elderly in rest homes, go to sporting events. I know it may sound a little weird, but one of the things I enjoy most is when we go downtown two or three times a month and help prepare food for the homeless. When you see people like that, you realize that there's more to life than hoops."

"Sounds kind of cool," Mitch said. "I thought all you guys did was sit around and read the Bible."

Cory smiled. "Well, we do that too, but you'd be surprised at how interesting that can be." He turned the wheel of his Mustang and rolled to a stop in Kenny Taylor's driveway. Parked cars lined both sides of the street. Kids talked and laughed in small groups on the front lawn and, even from the driveway, music could be heard coming from the house.

When Mitch and Cory walked through the

front door and into the living room, Mitch yelled, "Camden Rules!" and shouts went up from all over the house.

"Well, look who's here," Kenny Taylor said. "Glad you could make it, Web. That was a great shot!"

"If I could make three-point shots that easy every time," Cory said, "the college scouts would be offering me all kinds of stuff. I could have my pick—UCLA; Duke; Nevada, Las Vegas!"

Several other kids from school thumped Mitch and Cory on their backs. The whole basketball team was there—even the reserves. Cameron Lydell was talking to three kids about a new CD that was playing on the stereo. He was laughing about how he had stood in line at Tower Records for three hours to buy it. Six guys were playing half-court basketball out on the driveway. Cory looked around but didn't see any adults anywhere. *Maybe Taylor's parents are somewhere else in the house,* he guessed. A Domino's delivery person arrived with eight large pizzas, and everybody pitched in to help Taylor pay for them.

Taylor carried the pizzas to the dining room and laid them out on the table next to a roll of paper towels and some paper plates. A green Coleman ice chest stood on the floor next to the table, with the lid thrown open and chipped ice and soft-drink cans in it. Suddenly the dining room swarmed with kids. Cory slipped two slices of mushroom and olive onto a plate and pulled a can of Sprite out of the ice chest. He sat down on the arm of one of the chairs in the living room and took a couple huge bites of the pizza.

"Hey, Web, the hero of the game doesn't have to drink soda pop," Taylor said with a grin. "Here, have a cool one!" He tossed Cory an unopened can of beer.

Cory caught the can but put it on the floor next to him. "Uh, Sprite's just fine, Taylor. Thanks."

"What's the deal?" Taylor asked. "Don't you drink?"

To Cory it seemed as if everything that had been going on in the room stopped in a freeze-frame—all the talk and all the activity just stopped. Only the music continued on the stereo.

Cory shook his head. "No, I don't."

"Come on, dude," Taylor urged. "You've earned it. It's Miller time!"

"Yeah," Lydell added. "Lighten up, Web. Have some fun for a change!"

Then, unexpectedly, Mitch interrupted. "If Web doesn't want to drink," he said, "what's the big deal? In fact, maybe he knows something we don't. After all, he's the one who won the game for us today!" He sat down on the floor next to Cory.

Taylor stood in the doorway as if he had something more to say, but then turned and went back into the dining room. Several more kids came in from playing hoops on the driveway to get some pizza, and the party ignited again.

"Thanks," Cory said.

"Forget it," Mitch said. "I guess you don't drink because of your church, huh?"

"Yes and no," Cory said. "As I said before, I believe God gave me my abilities. If playing basketball is one of them, then I figure I should take care of my body."

"Makes sense, I guess," Mitch said. "Nothing wrong with pizza, is there?" He stuffed half a piece into his mouth at once.

Cory laughed. "Not that I know of," he said. He took several swallows of his Sprite. "Hey, Mitch. Our youth group is going to the Lakers game next Tuesday night. Why not come along?"

At first Cory thought Mitch hadn't heard him. He was just about to repeat himself.

"Sounds cool," Mitch said with a shrug. "Maybe I'll give it a try."

13 COMPARATIVE RELIGION

Pulling into the Safeway lot, I parked two or three places down from the store entrance. I don't know where he came from, but when I straightened up and closed the car door, I nearly ran right into a skinny, 20-something guy with an odd look of urgency in his eyes.

"Hi!" he said. "My name is Ron, and I'm giving away copies of this terrific book this afternoon. You may find it interesting." He thrust a shiny new paperback in my direction. On the cover appeared pictures of John Lennon and Swami Somebody-or-Other.

Usually I try to pass off this kind of encounter with a casual but firm "No thanks" and walk away. But today "spring was the mischief in me," as Robert Frost has said in a poem somewhere.

I leaned back against the door of my car and folded my arms, deciding for some unknown reason that now was the appropriate time for a little session in comparative religion—for me and for Ron of the Parking Lot. Two women passed by, looking nervously away as if they feared that Ron would lasso them into a conversation too. As we all know, one of our best defenses against such situations is never to make eye contact. They didn't, but one of them giggled and nudged the other.

As I casually paged through the book and glanced at the illustrations of fierce-looking superhuman creatures in otherworldly settings, Ron continued his pitch. "Do you have a religion?" he asked.

"Sure do," I said. "I'm a Seventh-day Adventist Christian."

"Far out!" Ron said. "You mean like the people at Ranch Apocalypse in Waco, Texas?"

"Uh, no—" I began, but Ron's attention was blindly marching on.

"You know," he said, "I believe that all religions are part of the greater cosmic truth. This book is really cool because it tells you in awesome detail how you can have a better life."

"What makes you think my life is so bad?" I asked.

Ron shrugged his shoulders, apparently not catching on to my playfulness. Obviously no sense of humor. "Just trying to be helpful," he said. "Our religion really offers some ways that you can make your experience even better on this great blue ball we share with one another. Surely everyone could improve things in life. For example, we believe that a vegetarian diet is the best thing for the human body."

Vegetarianism. Ah, yes! I smiled inwardly. Now there's a subject an Adventist can really sink his teeth into.

"You know," I said, "many Adventists feel exactly the same away about that. The Bible says that the human body is the temple of the Holy Spirit. God gave us stewardship over our bodies, and it's our responsibility as His created beings to take the best possible care of ourselves." I was determined to match Ron phrase for phrase and sentence for sentence with the things I'd learned back in Sabbath school. And not for nothing had I memorized all those key texts in Bible doctrines class.

"And, of course," Ron butted in, "another good reason for vegetarianism is that if we kill an animal we are killing another soul, just as if we were killing another human being. All animals have souls too, you see . . ."

He was really warming to his subject now. Snatching the knitted blue ski cap from his head, he punctuated his statements with a white-clenched fist. The late April wind ruffled his shoulder-length, dark brown hair. His lips were dry and chapped, and his eyes blinked irritably in the dry breeze.

Hadn't Elder Storz, our academy Bible doctrines teacher, once prophesied just such a confrontation as I was now involved in? I'd passed Bible docs without even looking back. But for some reason, this notion that animals have souls caught me way off base.

Several examples from the Bible came vaguely to mind of places where animals are said to have souls. Is this truly another reason that Adventists emphasize vegetarianism? I'd never heard it discussed before. And how do you argue an issue like this with someone you've just met by happenstance in a parking lot? Where do you start? And what sense would my comments make to someone who thinks the Bible is nothing more than just another book?

Fortunately—or maybe unfortunately—Ron wasn't going to give me a chance to develop a full answer anyway. "Tell you what," he said. "There's an address written down on the inside cover of that book. Why don't you come on by sometime, and we'll treat you to a real good vegetarian meal. Then we can talk over religion a little more." Visions of gongs and bells and bald, skinny priests in apricot robes loomed up in my mind. *What in the world would the food be like?* I wondered.

"Tell *you* what," I countered. "Give me your address, and I'll send you a book to read too."

"Just send it to that same address in there," Ron said. "I'll get it if you mail it to me there."

I nodded and then he was gone. Just like that! Already pulling another copy of the book out of his day pack, he had spotted another hapless victim getting out of a station wagon nearby.

As I turned toward the door into Safeway, I got to thinking that maybe I should have invited Ron to a good old SDA potluck. But he probably wouldn't have enjoyed it. No gongs and bells. No bald priests and no apricot robes. And we hardly ever talk religion at potlucks—or in parking lots either, for that matter.

14 MRS. MCKINLEY'S LIST

"Excuse me, young man. Would you be so kind as to help me with something?"

Trevor looked up from his half-completed film-processing envelope at the drug-store counter. A frail elderly lady stood next to him, so near, in fact, that she reminded him of a lost, clinging child. Thick glasses magnified her dark eyes to the size of fried eggs. "I can't see well since my operation," she said, "and I'm having trouble reading this label." Even her voice was thin. She thrust a brown bottle in his face. "Can you tell me if this is Milk of Magnesia?"

"Uh, no, ma'am," Trevor said, pulling the bottle back to a distance at which he could read it. "The label says this is hydrogen peroxide. I believe people use this stuff as an antiseptic or something."

"Oh, dear, that will never do," the lady said.

She squinted at the label on the bottle, her thin, gray hair stringing down in front of her face. "Where do you suppose they stock the Milk of Magnesia around this place?"

"I'm not sure," he said, looking around. "I don't work here."

"What's your point? Are you refusing to help me?"

"Well, no, ma'am. It's just that I thought you might have mistaken me for a store clerk."

"Anyone can see you're not a store clerk," the lady snapped. "What I *can't* see is the words on these labels. They deliberately print them small so you can't see them. Couldn't you take a couple minutes to help me find a bottle of Milk of Magnesia?"

"Sure," Trevor said with a sigh. It was becoming clear to him that he wasn't going to get out of Peoples Drug till this lady found what she was looking for. He pocketed his film-processing envelope and headed for the back of the store. "It's probably back there in aisle three among the health and beauty aids."

She shuffled hurriedly along beside him, laying her hand on his bare arm. It was as cool and light as a butterfly's touch. He caught a whiff of liniment. "I don't have much use for beauty aids anymore," she said, "but I can't go too long without Milk of Magnesia. It keeps me regular, you know, and when you get to be my age, you're willing to settle for regular."

Do I really need to be hearing this? Trevor wondered.

"I'm 87 years old, you know!" she said with just an air of pride.

It probably would hurt her feelings to know she looks more like 107, he thought, but decided not to mention it.

"Here we are," he said, reaching for a bottle. "What size do you want?"

"Economy size," she said. "I use a lot of the stuff. Constipation isn't any fun."

There she goes, he thought. *I don't really need all this information about her digestive system.*

"Anything I can help you with?" a pharmacist in a white lab coat asked from behind the two of them. It startled the old lady, and she nearly dropped the peroxide.

"Ooh, you frightened me," she said. "No, my grandson and I are doing just fine, thank you."

The pharmacist looked at Trevor a bit quizzically, then turned and passed on in a businesslike way down the aisle, whisking a feather duster here and there along the shelves. Trevor watched him till he was far enough away that he knew they wouldn't be overheard.

"Why did you call me your grandson?" he asked. "I've never seen you before in my life!"

She smiled. "I like to play pretend sometimes. Besides, I didn't think you'd mind."

"Well, now that you have your Milk of Magnesia, I guess I'll get back to the film counter."

"Oh, yes, by all means," she said. "We're all business now, aren't we? Actually, I also need some Ben-Gay, the stuff you rub on your aching joints. Makes them feel all warm and nice. Can't get by without it. If you help me find that, I'll set you free."

The Ben-Gay was on the shelf right behind

her. "Here it is," Trevor said, reaching around and handing it to her. She seemed almost disappointed that it was so near at hand, and he was a bit ashamed to realize at last what was going on. *Mr. Sensitivity: that's me!* he thought.

"Tell you what," Trevor said, "since you don't have any use for the hydrogen peroxide, *Grandma,* maybe we should put it back. Where did you get it?"

She smiled again, this time with just the slightest hint of mischief in her eyes. It made him feel as if he'd just been let in on a practical joke. "I have no idea," she said. "What row is this?"

He looked up at the poster hanging over the aisle. "This is row three," he said. "Come on, we'll take a look around."

They found the place for the hydrogen peroxide, as well as half a dozen other items she apparently considered absolutely essential. Trevor began to suspect that she was deliberately asking for an item that would be at the opposite end of the store from where they were standing, but by this time he'd become a willing player in her game.

At last he ushered her to the cash register, where she made her purchases. She fished the exact change out of her purse with surprising ease, and then headed for the exit.

"See you later, Grandma!" Trevor called.

" 'Bye," she said with a wave.

The pharmacist winked. "Not really your grandmother, is she?"

Trevor laughed. "No. How did you know?"

"That's Mrs. McKinley. She comes in here at least once a day and latches on to some poor, unsuspecting customer. Usually nobody will give her the time of day, but you seemed to be playing along so well that I didn't have the heart to say anything. Thanks for not complaining about her. Some people get really irritated and tell me we should shoo her out of here, like she's a public nuisance or something."

Trevor shrugged. "*Public* she is with a vengeance. *Nuisance?* I don't think so." He completed his film-processing envelope and handed it to the pharmacist with his roll of film in it. "Think Grandma will be here when I come back for these pictures?"

"Count on it," he said.

15 TRIBUTE TO MISS OLIVER

Tony was late for football practice or he'd have stopped. Besides, the mid-December morning was so cold you could see your breath, and he was afraid his 20-year-old Mustang would quit on him if he didn't keep riding the accelerator. Miss Oliver, who lived four houses down, was struggling with her garbage can, trying to stand it upright. It looked as though one of the dogs in the neighborhood had knocked it over and spilled cans and papers all over the sidewalk. It was a real mess.

"I'll help her next time," Tony muttered as he made the turn onto Baseline Boulevard.

Miss Oliver had retired two years before, when Tony was a freshman at San Bernardino High. She had taught English there for something like 40 years. Former students from all over the U. S. came to her tribute—a mayor, a police chief, a heart surgeon, two members of Congress, a newspaper editor, a famous defense lawyer, and even an astronaut. *In 40 years,* Tony mused, *I guess a good teacher can touch a lot of lives.*

Miss Oliver had been a neighbor on Loma Prieta Drive for as long as Tony could remember, so besides being one of the last 27 kids to take freshman English from her, he saw her almost every day in the neighborhood. He'd been impressed by all the attention she had received at her retirement ceremony. She even had her picture in the San Bernardino *Sun*. He figured that Miss Oliver was as close as he'd ever get to knowing someone famous.

But by the end of that first summer after her retirement, he hadn't given Miss Oliver another thought. He was going out for football, working at Walgreen's Drug Store, and trying to keep his Mustang running on used parts from the junkyard. Even Sundays didn't bring much spare time.

He'd completely forgotten about Miss Oliver and her garbage can by the time he arrived home from work at Walgreen's that night after dark. Mr. Pack, the assistant manager, had called in sick and Tony had been helping out in the parking lot, selling Christmas trees. He was an hour late getting home.

Before supper he went out to the garage to feed Sherbet, his 4-old golden Lab, but couldn't find her anywhere. He poured her a bowlful of Kibbles and filled her water bucket. Usually the sound of the Kibbles hitting the metal bowl was enough to bring her loping expectantly into the garage. But tonight Tony called and whistled—still no Sherbet.

So he walked down the driveway and out to the curb, looking up and down Loma Prieta. Sure enough, there was Sherbet with her whole head, shoulders, and two front feet inside Miss Oliver's empty garbage can, which lay on its side. Thinking he'd teach Sherbet a lesson about staying out of neighbors' garbage cans, he crossed the street and sneaked up behind her. She was busily lapping up something on the inside of the can and didn't hear him coming. With a playful swat on her hind quarters, he shouted, "Get out of that garbage can, you crazy mutt!"

Sherbet thumped her head like a bell clapper inside the can, yelped, and headed for home without looking back. Tony stood the can up, replaced the lid, and then decided to carry it around to the back of Miss Oliver's little place. No lights shone from the front of the house, giving it a cold, dark look of loneliness. Christmas lights outlined almost every other house on the block, and for the first time he realized that he couldn't remember ever seeing holiday decorations at Miss Oliver's house.

He didn't think she was home till he got back to the garage door. Then he noticed a single light on in the kitchen, throwing a four-paned patch of yellow light on the ground just outside. Miss Oliver appeared to be standing at the sink, washing dishes. Thinking she might mistake him for a prowler, he put the can down by the step and tapped on the back door. The porch light came on and Miss Oliver appeared in the doorway. A strand of unruly gray hair hung lifelessly down the right side of her face.

"Hi, Miss Oliver," Tony said. "I just brought

your garbage can up from the curb because I caught our dog in it. We'll try to keep an eye on her a little better so she doesn't knock it over anymore."

Miss Oliver blinked. "Thank you, young man. I greatly appreciate it. Do I know you from somewhere?"

"I'm Tony Jefferson from down the street. Don't you remember? I took freshman English from you a couple years ago at the high school. Diagramming sentences just about ruined my life!"

Recognition flickered across Miss Oliver's face. "Oh, yes, of course," she said. "I'm sorry I didn't recognize you at first. As I remember, you had a particularly difficult time with verbs, didn't you?"

"Verbs, nouns, interceptions, you name it!" Tony said with a grin.

Miss Oliver laughed.

"Hey," he continued without thinking, "why don't you have your Christmas decorations up?"

She ran a finger along the sill of the screen door. "Well, to tell you the truth, Tony, I'm not expecting anyone for Christmas; my only sister and her family live in Texas. It's very difficult for me to put up a tree by myself. I just can't get the hang of fastening that Christmas tree stand well enough. Last year's tree fell over three times. It seems I can't keep my Christmas trees *or* my garbage cans upright anymore. So I just thought maybe I'd not bother with holiday decorations this year. Doesn't that make me an awful Scrooge?"

Tony shrugged. "Not really, but it's a shame you don't have anyone to share the season with."

Miss Oliver smiled. "Oh, I have my cat and my records. Throughout the season I play the beautiful old Christmas carols nearly round the clock. I've almost worn them out, but I do enjoy them so."

"Well, Miss Oliver, I'd better get home for supper. Happy holidays!"

On his way back to the house he was thinking how sad it was that Miss Oliver couldn't get into the holiday spirit a little more. He remembered a scrawny tree at Walgreen's that he was sure no one would buy. Mr. Pack had threatened several times just to toss it into the dumpster at the back of the store, but he'd never got around to it. *Why not ask if he'd let me give it to Miss Oliver and help her decorate it?* Tony thought.

So after work the next day he asked Mr. Pack about it. He'd been helping to stock shelves in the store, so when he was ready to go home he stopped by the Christmas tree lot. "Where's that scrawny little tree we've had around for so long? You didn't sell it, did you?"

"Naw," Mr. Pack said. "I finally got tired of looking at it, so we burned it in the incinerator a couple hours ago. Figured it might as well provide us with a little warmth, if nothing else."

Tony had been thinking all afternoon how great it would be to surprise Miss Oliver with a Christmas tree and maybe help her set it up and decorate it. Now the tree wasn't there anymore. He pulled out his wallet and opened it: only $8 left till next payday.

"How much do you want for that five-footer?" he asked, pointing to a beautifully balanced blue spruce.

"What do you want with another tree?" Mr.

Pack asked. "You bought one and took it home for your parents a week ago."

"There's an elderly lady—Miss Oliver—who lives across the street from us. She doesn't have any decorations up, and I thought I'd give it to her and help her trim it."

"You mean Miss Oliver, the English teacher?" Mr. Pack asked.

"Yeah, do you know her?"

Mr. Pack smiled. "Sure do," he said. "Her American literature class was my favorite in high school 15 years ago." He looked at the tree. "It's a $20 tree," he said, "but I'll give it to you for $10."

"All I have is $8," Tony said.

"Close enough," Mr. Pack said. "And tell Miss Oliver Merry Christmas from me, will you?"

You should have seen the look on Miss Oliver's face when she first saw Tony standing on her front porch with a tree. For him it changed the meaning of Christmas forever.

16 MY WITNESS IN WORLD HISTORY

Pastor Randy told me there'd be days like this. Mrs. Alvarez handed me the six-page world history unit test on World War I, and the very first multiple-choice question showed that I was in big trouble. "Woodrow Wilson's plan for the League of Nations . . ."

Actually, it all started several weeks ago, after we'd been talking in our youth group about witnessing. "I know I'm supposed to be telling other people about Christ," I said, "but how does that work in school? As everybody knows, I'm the only member of our youth group at Paint Branch High. How am I supposed to go about witnessing there? I can't exactly ask for time to make a presentation during assembly. It would be the stoning of Stephen all over again!"

The youth group laughed because that's my real name—Stephen—just like the apostle.

"I think you're getting the wrong idea about witnessing, Steve," Pastor Randy said. "Jesus wasn't preaching *all* the time. In fact, He spent more time helping people than lecturing them. Just watch for a chance to be helpful to others, and sooner or later people will begin to notice that you're not the typical teenager, that there's something different about you. Opportunities to share your faith will crop up before you know it. Just hang in there."

So I decided I'd try to be the most helpful kid at Paint Branch High. The good Samaritan wasn't going to have anything on me! I signed up to tutor other kids in mathematics, the only subject I'm really comfortable in. I joined the Environmental Club and spent one evening a week with a bunch of kids on campus clean-up projects—believe me, Paint Branch can use it. I contributed $10 to a fund someone was taking up for a sophomore who needs a kidney transplant. I carried books, opened doors, collected papers, and cleaned up after food fights in the cafeteria.

And nothing happened. Zilch! Nobody seemed to notice. I might as well have been doing all this stuff on Neptune. And, to tell the truth, all my helpfulness projects were beginning to affect my grades a little bit.

I looked up from my world history test. You know you're in trouble when the teacher has left half a page for an essay question that you've answered in two lines. Marsha Detwiler, sitting in the desk to my left, was wearing out her pencil on *her* essay questions.

Marsha is hard to figure. She always scores among the top two or three in the two classes we have in common: world history and American literature. And she often asks really deep questions that leave the rest of us scratching our heads. Yet she's anything but the buttoned-down high achiever that you'd expect. She wears a ring in her left nostril, frumpy clothes, and black leather combat boots. Yes, I said *combat boots.*

I don't really know Marsha very well. Kids say her home life has been really lousy, that her father abandoned his family when Marsha was 2 years old, and that her mother is an alcoholic. I've always felt a little ill at ease around her. I think everybody does. She's friendly enough, but it's just that she seems to come from a world that is so different from my own. In fact, she appears to think it's important to be different.

She glanced up in my direction, and I guess she could see that I was obviously in trouble. She smiled a little, pushed her test to the corner of her desk nearest me, and nonchalantly stretched her arms straight out over her head and yawned. She writes in such huge lettering that anyone within three rows could have read the answers on her test. For just a moment it looked as though I might be able to improve the score on my test by 15 or 20 percentage points. The answers were there for the taking, and Mrs. Alvarez was completely lost in her copy of *Time* magazine.

But I knew I could never bring myself to take answers from Marsha's test. I smiled and shook my head and turned my test over, laying it face down in front of me. In the stillness of the classroom I didn't dare try to explain, even though I knew Marsha probably wouldn't understand why I didn't take her up on her gesture.

After the bell rang, I turned in my test with a sigh and headed for my locker down by the biology lab. World history is my last class of the day, and I needed to get my jacket and a couple books before I left for home. Just as I slammed the locker door shut, I turned and nearly ran into Marsha.

She cocked her head a little and looked at me with a quizzical expression. "What's the deal, Steve? You trying to tell me you didn't need a little help on that test?"

I laughed. "No, Marsha, I needed *a lot* of help."

"So why didn't you take some of my answers? You afraid you're going to mess up the bell curve or something?"

"Uh, it's a little hard to explain," I said.

Marsha folded her arms in front of her and peered at me through her John Lennon glasses. "Try," she said.

"Well, I think it's kind of important to earn my grades myself. That's the way I've been brought up. It just isn't real honest to take answers from someone else."

"Even if it means you'll flunk a unit test in world history?"

"I probably won't flunk the test," I said with a shrug. "I usually squeak by with at least a C. But even if I didn't pass, there are other things in this world that are more important."

"You know what I think?" Marsha said. "I think you're weird."

I glanced at the ring in Marsha's left nostril but decided not to explore with her the idea of a girl in combat boots thinking *I* am weird. She must have read my thoughts.

"Tell me this, Steve. Why haven't you ever asked me why I wear a ring in my nose? It seems to be a humongous subject of fascination to just about everyone else around here."

"Why *do* you wear it?" I asked.

"Just trying to make a statement," she said. "Isn't that pretty much what you were doing by not taking answers off my world history exam—trying to make a statement?"

"Well, yeah," I said. "I guess I was—in a way."

"Yeah," she said. "I guess you were. And that's OK, Steve, because most of the losers in this school don't have anything unique to say, you know what I mean? They're all trying to sing off the same page."

I wish I could say that the real meaning of Marsha's comment sank in immediately, but it didn't till I was thinking about it at home that evening. In her own way she was telling me that she'd noticed my efforts to witness at Paint Branch High—at least in world history class. It made me feel pretty good. Pastor Randy told me there'd be days like this.

17 HANDCUFFED!

Sooner or later, most of us have read the book *A Tale of Two Cities* in an English class. It begins with words that go something like this: "It was the best of times, it was the worst of times." I remember thinking *How can something be the best and the worst? It just doesn't make any sense!* Now I know what the writer meant.

I always look forward to the Fourth of July each year. Parades, swimming, ball games, picnics, fireworks—the people here in Los Robles go all out. When those guys back in 1776 got the whole thing started by declaring independence, it's like they must have had me particularly in mind. Nobody enjoys fireworks more than I do.

That's why, in fact, I found myself in handcuffs in the back of a police car one July Fourth, parked at the edge of a smoldering field of grass. Firefighters trained plumes of water on the blackened field and on what was left of the board fence that had once separated the Stater Brothers grocery store from the vacant lot behind it.

I sat there slumped over, with my forehead resting on the back of the seat in front of me, staring at my shoes and fighting to keep from breaking down. The handcuffs bit into my wrists, turning my fingers blue, and although the engine and air conditioner in the squad car were running, sweat trickled down my neck and forehead. My heart was thumping like a pile driver, and I thought I was going to pass out. The best day of the year had turned into a nightmare. The only positive thing I could think of was that the fire hadn't damaged Stater Brothers.

The squad car shook suddenly as the officer swung open the front door on the driver's side and sat down heavily behind the wheel. He was as big as a pro linebacker, with a scowl on his face and hair that was almost white. Tossing a clipboard on the seat next to him, he turned around to look at me. "You OK?"

I nodded my head weakly, still not at all sure I was going to keep from throwing up. People stood around on the sidewalk, watching the firefighters as they soaked the vacant lot with water, eyeing me curiously as if I were a caged animal of some kind. The manager of the Stater Brothers store, hands on his hips, was talking to one of the firefighters, pointing at me and shouting something I couldn't quite make out. His face was red right up to the top of his bald head, and the veins on his neck bulged as he shook a finger in the face of the firefighter.

The officer in the front seat picked up the clipboard again and pulled a pencil from behind his ear. "Where are your parents today, kid?"

"My dad's in Chicago this week on business and won't be back till Sunday. Mom is on duty until 11:00 over at Riverside County Hospital. She's a nurse."

"So, you're on your own today, looking for some buildings to burn down or something? The fireworks program down by Lake Elsinore tonight just isn't enough excitement for you?"

"It was an accident," I protested. "I was just playing around with some firecrackers—"

"You're aware, I assume, that firecrackers are prohibited in Riverside County?" the officer interrupted as he scribbled something down on the clipboard.

"Yes, sir, but everybody has them! I'm not the only one."

"Well, son, unfortunately if everyone has them, you're the only one who has nearly set fire to Stater Brothers. People sometimes wonder why laws are made against such things as firecrackers. What's the big deal, right? The problem is that we don't always get the fires put out before they cause some big-time damage. And people sometimes get hurt—and killed. The laws are meant to prevent those kinds of things from happening."

"I never meant any harm, Officer. It's the Fourth of July, and I was just playing around."

"I understand that, young man, but now you're going to have to figure the cost of 'just playing around.' The weeds and stuff in this vacant lot aren't much of a loss, of course. No one can be worried about the value of that. But there's a $500 fine for illegal fireworks here in Los Robles, and then, of course, there's the cost of replacing that fence."

I felt suddenly dizzy, and a wave of nausea washed over me again. *There's no place in the world that I can get money like that,* I thought. *What're they going to do to me for this?*

Without another word the officer got out of the car and walked over to where the Stater Brothers' manager was standing. I watched intently as they spoke to one another, the officer towering over the manager, but couldn't make out exactly what they were saying. The manager looked at me a couple times, but by now he seemed to be calming down a little. Finally, shaking his head, he stomped off toward the truck loading ramp at the back of the grocery store.

The officer returned to the car, this time getting in the back seat across from me. "Listen, kid, here's the deal. The store manager, Mr. Mariana, has cooled down quite a bit. You gave him a pretty bad scare, but he says you didn't really cause a great deal of harm, considering. He says the fence was pretty run down anyway. So we can forget about any damage that you may have done to property.

"But there's still the problem that you've broken the law." He sat a moment, chewing on the eraser of his pencil. "Here's what I'm going to do. It's important for you to realize that I *could* take you down to police headquarters, contact your parents, and fill out a complete report that would make it necessary for you and your parents to appear in court and pay a whopping fine. That's what the law would allow me to do."

Then he looked directly at me, and for the first time it dawned on me that the situation I'd put myself in on that hot afternoon in early July had affected *him* in some unexplainable way. The man who sat in that official uniform across the seat from me was concerned about more than mere law enforcement.

"I'm going to let you off this time with a warning," he said at last, reaching for my wrists with the key to the handcuffs.

I'll never be able to describe exactly the feelings that I had when the officer removed those handcuffs and I opened the door to the squad car. As I walked the four blocks home, I felt as though I'd stepped from a shadow as cold and dark as stone into the inviting sunlight of a second chance that I knew I didn't deserve. It was the worst *and* the best Fourth of July of my life!

18 NO GREEN THUMB

Mrs. Valenti lived across the street in a little house and yard that seemed to fit her personality—fussy. A man came once a week to mow her lawn, which always looked like a putting green. And her flower beds, laid out in smooth, even rows, seemed to be blooming year-round. Daisies, zinnias, and mums took their turns right on cue through spring, summer, and fall.

And when an occasional softball rolled into her flower beds from a street game among the neighborhood kids, the kids usually came to Kyle's front door to have him ask Mrs. Valenti for the return of their ball.

"Why don't you go yourself?" Kyle always asked with a smile.

"You're older," they'd say, "and we're scared of her."

So Kyle had discovered that when you got to know her, Mrs. Valenti wasn't really all that bad. She just knew how she wanted things in her yard, and softballs weren't part of the plan.

Then one summer day she motioned for Kyle to come over for a talk, and she looked as if she had something pretty important on her mind. She was sitting in her squeaky wicker rocking chair on the front porch.

"Hello, Mrs. Valenti," he said. "Been a pretty hot day, hasn't it?"

"Oh, not too bad. I wonder if you'd do me a favor."

"I'll try," he said. "What do you need?"

"I'm going to visit my son in Oregon for three weeks, and I need someone to watch the house for me—take in the mail and water the house plants, things like that. I've already arranged to leave Fred with Mrs. Wagner down the block, so you won't have to worry about him."

Kyle looked through the window at the green parrot cracking sunflower seeds in its cage. *How,* he wondered, *did Mrs. Valenti ever decide on* Fred *as a name for a bird?* With a loud squawk, Fred tilted his head to the right and eyed him suspiciously. "Sure, Mrs. Valenti," Kyle said, "I'll be glad to watch the house for you."

Four days later, on the evening before she was to leave, he reported back for his instructions.

"Come on in," she said, swinging the screen door outward toward him.

He wiped his feet on the mat and entered Mrs. Valenti's world. He could see his face in her shiny hardwood floors. Plants were everywhere: on the mantelpiece, the kitchen windowsill, the dining-room table, the piano—anywhere light could get to them. The house smelled fresh as a flower shop.

"If the weather isn't too hot," she began, "you'll have to water the plants only once a week. And whatever you do, *don't overwater them!*"

"I'll be very careful, Mrs. Valenti."

"This one is my pride and joy," she said, lightly touching the branch of a plant standing in the living-room window. "It's a *Ficus benjamina.*" She said it as if it should somehow mean something special to Kyle. "Be sure to watch it especially."

He nodded and promised to be faithful in caring for the plants. *How much trouble can a bunch of plants be?* he thought.

But within four days after Mrs. Valenti had left, the *Ficus benjamina* seemed to be drooping a little. *If it's droopy, it obviously needs water,* he reasoned. So he gave the soil a good soaking. Before the first week ended, leaves were dropping off. They were still green and showed no signs of pests, but they were falling like snowflakes. Every day when he checked the house, the floor under the *Ficus benjamina* was strewn with leaves. He picked them up each day, hoping they would be the last—that the plant would take a turn for the better. But with only two days before Mrs. Valenti's return, her *Ficus benjamina* looked like a dead stick.

He was even present to witness the falling of the last leaf. He guessed the draft from opening the door blew it off. It gently floated to the floor.

That evening at the dinner table Kyle's father

mentioned the family picnic they'd been planning for the coming Sunday afternoon. "If you want to invite a friend along," his mother told Kyle, "we'll have plenty of food."

Though he'd heard what his mother had said, he'd been thinking about the *Ficus benjamina* and didn't respond.

"Earth to Kyle!" his father said.

"Sorry," Kyle said. "I'm looking forward to the picnic, but for now, I'm in a real bind. I've been taking care of Mrs. Valenti's house plants, and her favorite one just gave up the ghost this afternoon. If she doesn't like the kids' softball in her pansies, she'll probably have a heart attack when she sees her dead plant."

To make matters worse, the *Ficus benjamina* could be clearly seen in Mrs Valenti's front window. Whenever the neighborhood kids saw Kyle, they shook their heads. "Oh, man," they said, "are you going to get it when Mrs. Valenti gets home!"

"Yeah," he said. "I know!"

On the morning she returned, he gave her a couple hours to get settled before going over to see her. He'd decided to face the problem squarely. So he crossed the street and rang the doorbell.

Getting no answer, he rapped on the screen door. Still not a sound, so he quietly pushed the door open. Mrs. Valenti was sitting on the sofa in her living room. She looked lost in thought.

"Mrs. Valenti," he said, "did you hear me knock?"

She drew in a deep breath and looked at him as if she had just wakened. "I'm sorry," she said. "Please come in."

He stepped inside the living room, leaving the door open.

"What happened to my *Ficus?*" she asked.

"I don't know, Mrs. Valenti. Honest, I gave it my very best care, but from the day you left, it just seemed to go downhill."

"Are you expecting that I'll get after you the way I do the neighborhood ballplayers?"

"Well, I know you might be upset with me. I know how much the plant meant to you."

Mrs. Valenti looked at Kyle, her gray eyes softer than he'd ever noticed them before. "I'll tell you something," she said. "My plants are really all I have. My son and daughter-in-law live a thousand miles away, and neighbors just aren't neighborly anymore. I don't even know the name of the people in that yellow house next to yours, and they moved in last April or so. My plants are just about the only things that know I'm here—except for Fred, of course." The green parrot cast a cross look at the mention of his name.

For the first time in the two years since Kyle's family had moved into the house on Springfield Drive, he was close enough to Mrs. Valenti to notice the lines of loneliness in her face.

"I'll tell you what," he said. "Our family is going on a picnic to Morgan Park next Sunday. It may not make up for the *Ficus,* but would you like to come along?"

She smiled a little slyly. "You know," she said. "You may not know much about taking care of plants. But you definitely have a talent for taking care of people."

19 THE WORLD'S SHORTEST MISSION TRIP

"Passengers holding tickets for Southwest Airlines flight 103 for Mexico City are now boarding the aircraft through gate B-24."

Melissa fought back the tears and gave her best friend, Rene, one last hug. Then Rene, too choked up to speak, turned and headed for the jetway.

"Sure wish you were going along," Colin said, punching Melissa playfully on the shoulder. "We're going to miss you."

"Yeah," Patrice said, "it just doesn't seem right that we're all going to be able to go on this great mission trip, and you're going to have to stay behind after all."

"Especially since you are the one who organized the whole thing," Carlos added.

"Just couldn't come up with the money to pay

for it," Melissa said with a brave smile. "Have a really good time, you guys! You can tell me all about it when you get back."

Moments later she was waving as the last of the 14 members of her youth group disappeared through gate B-24. She stood alone and tried to see if anyone would wave to her from one of the windows on the plane, but the slant of the sun turned all the windows to mirrors. "So, everybody is going to Mexico for spring vacation to work in an orphanage," she muttered, shaking her head, "and I'm not even going across town! Who's better at working with kids than I am?"

She thought of the three McAllister children, whom she cared for every afternoon till their mother arrived home from work. She met them at school, herded them the seven blocks home, helped them to complete their homework, if they had any, and prepared their supper, day in and day out. A couple months back she'd even led them on a hair-raising expedition one afternoon to the mall to select a birthday gift for their mother. When they'd arrived home with it, 7-year-old Kenny had insisted on wrapping it all by himself—a little colored paper and probably 20 feet of tape. But for days after, the kids had talked about how they'd surprised their mother.

At the thought of the McAllister kids, Melissa remembered suddenly that she had only about half an hour before she had to pick them up at school, so she immediately headed for the parking garage. Mr. Matthews, the youth director for her church, had asked her to drive his van home after bringing the gang to the airport. He'd told Melissa she could pick up the McAllister kids on the way back.

But all the way into town traffic was unusually heavy and the drivers discourteous. It all seemed to suggest the congestion and frustration in Melissa's life. She drove rather mechanically and fumed about the unfairness of not being able to go on the mission trip to Mexico. *Ever since I was 5 years old and heard that returned missionary tell about his adventures in Papua New Guinea,* she thought, *I've wanted to do something for God's work in some exotic, foreign country. So here I am in Denver, and the only exotic thing I ever have to face is helping Kenny McAllister when he locks himself in the bathroom.*

But she smiled just a bit as Kenny came into view, standing with his two older brothers on the porch in front of Aurora Elementary School. "There they are as usual," she muttered. "They don't call themselves the three stooges for nothing."

Because they were used to walking home, the McAllister kids didn't at first realize who Melissa was, waving at them from the bright-red van at the curb of the parking lot in front of the school. But then they raced across the lawn toward her. Michael, the eldest, reached the van first, claiming squatter's rights to the front seat next to Melissa.

"I get to ride shotgun!" he shouted triumphantly.

Kenny dropped his jacket and had to go back for it. He was sweaty and disgusted by the time he got to the van and stomped off toward the very back seat.

"Cool van," Terrance said from the seat behind Melissa. "Did you steal it?"

"Yeah, right," Melissa snickered. "It belongs

to Mr. Matthews, our youth director at church. I have to return it to his house after your mother gets home tonight. We used it to take a bunch of kids to the airport so they could go on a mission trip to Mexico over spring vacation."

"Mexico? Cool! Why didn't you go?" Terrance asked.

"I wish!" Melissa said.

"No kidding," Michael pressed, "didn't you want to go with your friends to Mexico?"

"Of course I did. But my family is as broke as yours is," Melissa said, a little more bitterly than she knew she should have. *Why on earth*, she wondered, *am I sharing this with three little kids who have no clue what I'm talking about?*

"What would we do if you went to Mexico?" Kenny asked. "Couldn't you just be kind of a missionary to our house?"

"Yeah," Terrance added. "We could maybe act uncivilized or something."

"Oh, that would be a stretch," Melissa said with a smile. "You guys wouldn't have to do much acting in a role like that!" She glanced back in the rearview mirror at Kenny, who was having a difficult time with his seat belt. "Out of the mouths of babes . . . ," she said.

Kenny's head jerked up, and he shot back a defiant look. "I ain't no baby," he said with a scowl.

"No," Melissa said, shaking her head, "you surely are not, Kenny. In fact I think you've got a much better grip on what it means to be a missionary than I do."

20 THE TWO ENVELOPES

Ian was sitting cross-legged on his bed when Marcus arrived. When you get to know Ian, you soon learn that he's likely to be coming out of left field with another of his half-baked ideas. But this immediately appeared to be a different situation.

"What's the deal?" Marcus asked. "You made this sound like an emergency. What's so important that it couldn't wait till I see you in school tomorrow?"

Ian looked vacantly around his room, his eyes as wide as campaign buttons. A soft gurgling sound came from the algae-coated aquarium under the window. "Shut the door behind you," he said, a trace of something awestruck in his voice.

Marcus kicked a baseball glove and a small pile of clothes out of the way and pushed his bedroom door closed. "All right, Ian. What's going on?"

Ian chewed his lip thoughtfully and looked down at two unopened envelopes lying in front of him on the rumpled orange bedspread. One looked like an average business letter; the other, on more personal-appearing lavender stationery, carried the name Naomi Sendak in scratchy lettering over the return address in the corner. Marcus sat down on the foot of the bed.

"You know," Ian said, pointing to a newspaper section lying folded in half next to where Marcus was sitting, "I've been kind of experimenting with that horoscope column in the LA *Times*, trying to see if there's anything to it. Well, this morning's paper said that if I was born under the sign of Capricorn, I'd receive a letter today that would change my life."

Marcus rolled his eyes. "Ian, you have way too much spare time on your hands! You know how I feel about this stuff. Can you actually sit there and believe that every Capricorn on earth is going to get a life-changing letter today? I mean, think about it: we're not talking here about subtle little everyday things; we're talking *life-changing* stuff—for every last Capricorn from here to Calcutta!"

"Well, I kind of thought that this particular forecast may have been intended only for readers of the *Times*. That would narrow it down quite a bit, wouldn't make it have to be so—'cosmic.'"

"Astrology is *supposed* to be cosmic," Marcus reminded him. "It claims that the movement of the stars in the cosmos—millions of light-years away—somehow influences our everyday lives here on earth. So now you think that the stars have a special relationship with the people of Los Angeles?"

"I can't explain exactly how the law of gravity works either," Ian shot back, "but that doesn't mean it doesn't exist. What's important is if it works. All I know is that I can go months at a time without getting anything in the mail—not even a Damark catalog—but now on the same day my horoscope talks about a life-changing letter, I get two things in the mail."

"Ooh!" Marcus said. "Doesn't it just give you goose bumps?"

But he knew that sarcasm just didn't work with Ian. Never had. He'd tried it before. When you got to know this guy, he'd decided, you soon learned that the only way out is through. Like being placed in the middle of a swamp, you have to slog your way through the muck and the alligators. You might as well just wade in.

"So which of those two letters is going to change your life?" Marcus asked with a sigh.

Ian grinned. "Not sure, but who knows? Maybe one of them is really important."

"All right," Marcus said. "I give up. Let's open them up so you'll know what new direction your life is going to take and then I can go home. I don't know why you always try to rope me into these weird experiments of yours. Last month it was UFOs, and before that the Loch Ness monster. Why me?"

"That's easy," Ian said. "You're my friend." He tore the business envelope open, tossed it toward the already overflowing wastebasket in the corner, and began to read the letter: "Dear Occupant: It is with great pleasure . . ."

"Wait a minute, Ian. '*Dear Occupant*'? This

letter isn't even addressed to you personally."

"Well, yeah," he said, "but even without opening it, Mom and Dad said they didn't want it. I have to be ready for every possibility, don't I?" Holding up his hand to cut Marcus off, he finished reading the letter aloud. For $35 a month, a beneficiary would receive a million dollars if "Occupant" died of cancer or got hit by a truck.

"Hey," Marcus said, "there's an idea. You can name me your beneficiary, and at least someone's life may be changed!"

"Very funny!"

Ian tossed the letter toward the wastebasket, then tore into the smaller, lavender envelope.

"Who's Naomi Sendak?" Marcus asked.

"My grandmother," he said. "She lives in Florida, and I hear from her maybe only a couple times a year—Christmas and my birthday."

"Well, your birthday's what, three or four months away, and Christmas way beyond that."

He read the letter aloud. It spoke of lumbago ("back's so bad I can hardly get around anymore"), and the weather ("hot as a 'depot stove'"), and the rising costs of prescription medicine ("what're those insurance companies trying to do to me?"), and the noise of a neighbor's stereo system ("I've called the police out four times, but they don't care!"). Nothing even remotely connected with *anything* in Ian's life, much less a life-changing impact. The two friends looked at each other for a long moment.

Marcus picked up the newspaper section, absent-mindedly scanning the horoscope column. "This thing's written by somebody named Dr. E. K. Oo," he said. "Doesn't a name like that alone make you wonder a little bit? I don't even know how to pronounce it."

"Hey," Ian said, "this guy predicted the last California earthquake, the last four presidential elections, and the breakup of Charles and Di. Why do you have to be such a Philistine about this stuff?"

"Philistine! Ever since we first got to know each other in algebra class a year ago I've been trying to get you to attend one of our youth meetings at church, and you've always refused because you say Christianity is just a lot of 'superstition.' And now you're calling *me* a Philistine!"

Marcus was still scanning the horoscope column, and it took a moment or two to sink in, but slowly he realized that something wasn't quite right. "Wait a minute, Ian. You read this thing all wrong. The life-changing letter is supposed to come to the people under the sign of Sagittarius, not Capricorn."

"Get out of here!" he said.

"No kidding," Marcus said, laughing. "You read the wrong horoscope!"

Ian pushed his glasses up, lost in thought momentarily. His forehead wrinkled and his eyebrows rose. "What *does* it say, then, about Capricorn?"

Marcus looked him squarely in the eye. Crumpling up the newspaper section, he tossed it directly at Ian, bouncing it off his head. "It says if you don't wise up, a friend is going to make you see stars that don't appear on any astrology chart!"

"Ah," Ian said with a smile, "now there's some advice that makes some sense."

"Yeah," Marcus said. "It isn't in the form of a letter, but it just may change your life!"